Praise for *A Knit of Identity*

"With *A Knit of Identity* Chris Motto has accomplished something both astonishing and profound. Against the backdrop of professions as seemingly ordinary as truck driving and road laying, Motto has crafted one of the most unique and uniquely moving love stories I have ever read, featuring what might be the two most memorable lead characters in literary history. Haunted by their separate pasts and struggling to find places in a world from which there are painfully, even physically, alienated, they encounter each other in the unlikely locale of a South Carolina trucker bar. What happens between them changes them forever and will change the reader as well, who is forced, by the beauty of the relationship and the passion in Motto's writing, to rethink every gender category they may have held dear. Motto shows us that truly love is all that matters. As much her characters learn this, the reader will learn it doubly. And it's a lesson we can't absorb enough. *A Knit of Identity* will make of every reader a different and wiser and nobler person."

- John Vanderslice, author of *Nous Nous*

"This hard-scrabble novel was difficult to put down. It's an old-fashioned American love story. Motto writes with the conviction that these people's stories really matter. Her characters seem driven by a gathering need to learn and do what is right. *A Knit Of Identity* opens new windows to the dark corners of the human heart and spirit where real loses and real gains are made. It's genuinely moving."

- Lisa Cupolo, author of *Have Mercy On Us*

A Knit of Identity

Chris Motto

Regal House Publishing

Published by
Regal House Publishing, LLC
Raleigh, NC 27605
All rights reserved

ISBN -13 (paperback): 9781646032778
ISBN -13 (epub): 9781646032785
Library of Congress Control Number: 2021949163

Interior and cover design by Lafayette & Greene
Cover images © by C. B. Royal

Regal House Publishing, LLC
https://regalhousepublishing.com

The following is a work of fiction created by the author. All names, individuals, characters, places, items, brands, events, etc. were either the product of the author or were used fictitiously. Any name, place, event, person, brand, or item, current or past, is entirely coincidental.

Printed in the United States of America

For Shawn, who carries my heart,
and for Francie, who keeps it beating

synchronicity
meaningful coincidence without apparent cause

There's a myth that truck drivers take seriously and it's this: if you see the black dog when you're driving, something bad is about to happen. It isn't a superstition nearly as well-mannered as the black cat. If a black cat crosses your path, you have options, an automatic opportunity to change your fate. It's the only superstition I can think of that offers a warning and a choice. Not so with the black dog. Once you see it, you have somewhere between zero and five seconds to react. Usually it's closer to zero, and your reaction will affect what happens to the eighty-four thousand pounds of rolling iron riding your ass.

Many acquaintances of mine have seen it, but I've lost just one friend to it. People wonder how I know he saw the black dog before he died. For now, I can offer only this: I just do. His name was Bobby and he was making a run through Tennessee, hauling a load of aluminum down seven winding miles of Jellico Mountain. Its drop in elevation is hazardous, it's liable to be seventy degrees at one end and freezing sleet at the other, and it curves so Z-like that between the speed and the height it can eat up a set of brakes as fast as a shark can detect blood. Accidents on Jellico Mountain, both four wheeler and big truck, are as commonplace as falling leaves in autumn. Crosses could fill the roadside if anyone cared enough to put them there.

We lose somewhere close to a thousand truckers a year to accidents. You'd think we'd learn from their mistakes. We know we need to keep our wits about us and stay awake, but it's impossible not to memorize stretches of road. One thing's for certain: We learn quickly we shouldn't take for granted the mountainous areas. What we do with that knowledge is up to us.

When I started driving, I was a fresh twenty-one-year-old who didn't have much going for me. I knew nothing about everything. My first run was from New York to Florida, nearly fourteen hundred miles, and I walked away from it still knowing nothing. Bobby once told me you're not a driver until you've been through your first accident and seen the damage. Like a virgin, I was afraid of the pain, but I couldn't wait for it to happen.

I may not have been a real driver when I first started, but I couldn't help but feel like God sitting in that rig. She was as old and as rickety as a locomotive, but she was known for her long runs and durability, her power. I loved her; she was my first. I named her Big Bertha. I made the beginning of that run in eleven hours, stopping at a truck stop in Charlotte, North Carolina—Queen City as we call it—for my first official dinner as a trucker. It wasn't easy walking into a truck stop as a woman (hell, a kid, really), when nearly all its patrons were men, when the only women they saw back then were either Lot Lizards who gave a whole new name to parking lot screwing, or fluffy haired coeds who hopped out of their boyfriends' sports cars or gripped on to each other for dear life as they half ran, half walked to the bathroom because they couldn't hold it long enough to find a respectable rest area. When a woman like that walks into a truck stop, just about everyone stops to watch the ass saunter by. It doesn't matter if you're a man or a woman, married or single, gay or straight. You're used to watching the tail of cars and trucks, not a mound of flesh. By force of nature, you look. It was going to happen to me whether I wanted it to or not. I took a deep breath and pushed through the door, zeroing in on the counter. As expected, they looked, until they noticed the work boots, the oil-stained jeans. Just like that it didn't matter what my ass looked like, it wasn't royal enough to sit upon one of their thrones.

Paranoia sat in my gut like the bricks I was carrying. I couldn't hide the fact that I wanted to be accepted—any respect would have to wait for time and experience, and that I understood. But it was too depressing to think about being turned away from another thing I was really good at, all because of my gender.

There were quite a few lady truckers out there, but just enough to irritate the masses, not enough to make a stand.

I ordered the most masculine entrée I could find—steak and potato—and stared at the soap swirls in the cup of black coffee. I pretended not to hear the whistles, the sarcastic kisses, the catcalls. The sounds weren't exactly aimed at me. They certainly were about me but directed to each other loud enough for me to hear. I made the choice not to turn and tell them off. I was twenty-one, what could I say? It was a thin line I was walking. I didn't want to be too assertive or defensive, nor did I want to seem like a coward. I'd defend myself only if I were directly challenged. I listened to them heckle for as long as it took to finish my brew. Heckles that stung like razor-sharp pellets. I'm not one to carry the past with me, but it was difficult not to compare it to the laughter from the girls in high school. Insecurity began to resurface. But before it could drain me of my contentment, the waitress, carrying a full pot, went over to a table, pulled the baseball hat off one man's head and hit him with it. She said something like, "Why don't you save it for the strip joint."

Then she came over to pour me another and gave me a wink. It lifted my spirits a little. I thought maybe she'd talk to me, but that's when Bobby came in, and she said sort of off-hand, "Well, hello, darlin'. Where you been at? Haven't seen you in a dog's age." He answered with a wave and sat down next to me. No one else would. He greeted me with a nod, asked me who I was, and held out a light instead of a hand. I hadn't even gotten the cigarette out of the pack. The other truckers watched this exchange from beneath the bills of their caps.

"Danny," I mumbled, and waited for a snide remark about my name.

"How long you been at it?" he asked, apparently unaffected.

"This is my first run," I said sheepishly, tapping off a non-existent ash.

"That's quite an antique you ridin'. It looks a bit big for someone who ain't got a pair of balls."

It came out sounding affectionate rather than derogatory, but any word related to male anatomy made men of all ages laugh. A guy at the register decided to be a smart aleck. He muttered, "The pickle park is a few miles back, missy." He didn't think I'd know that a pickle park was a rest area where the hookers hung out, but I had learned the language from days on the road with my father. The driver got his laugh. Then he said louder, "The only thing that girl should be riding is my dick."

They haw hawed into their beer bottles and coffee cups. I nodded, even smiled. Sat up nice and straight, sticking out what very little I had up there, showing them I was proud to be a woman, and turned my stool to get a good look at the testosterone behind me. I gave each of them an artificial glance, so they knew I wasn't that interested, except for the one at the register. I slid off the stool and walked up to him. He wasn't that much taller than me, but beefier with a smell like rancid fruit. As I approached, he turned to me, leaning into my space, hoping, maybe, I was going to take him up on his offer. My hand shot out too quick for him to react, and like a K9, I latched onto the crotch of his pants, gripping his balls like fruit about to be savagely plucked from a tree. I sized him up good before releasing him.

"You couldn't pay me enough, *good buddy*," I answered, deliberately using the term that over the years had changed from comrade to homosexual. Now I got the laughs, and perhaps a tiny bit of respect. Even though my heart was pounding, I strolled casually back to my stool and said to Bobby, "From the feel of things I got bigger balls than some."

Bobby looked around at the laughing men. "Hell, I could of saved you the walk and told you that myself."

I hadn't planned on spending the night at the truck stop, but Bobby said I looked tired and convinced me to stay. Told me I reminded him of his daughters. Wondered aloud why I wasn't working in an office or married to a nice boy, like his girls. We left our trucks at the stop and crossed the street to a bar. It was here Bobby initiated me into the world I believed in due time would lead me to wherever it was I was supposed be. He told me about the black dog, not knowing it would get him three years later, or that five months after that another trucker would, like a corner shot, cross a median and take my parents out too. Bobby described the dog, best he could, as a vicious Doberman, his yellow teeth snarling, his eyes black as night. The grim reaper of truckers, Bobby joked. And that's why, in the end, Bobby convinced me to stay over; don't ever give the black dog a chance at you, he said, if you can help it. He didn't seem nearly as afraid of it as he wanted me to be, and I wondered if after so many years of driving, you got to the point where you felt untouchable, infallible even. Or if you just stopped caring.

He told me that if I stayed at it long enough, my truck would take me just about everywhere, including the other side, and since we all had to go eventually, what better way? But he told me other things that night too. Some about safety and brotherhood, but the stories always came back to the coincidental, the bizarre, the urban legends. He took them all seriously when he spoke of them.

"There was this one trucker who rear ended a station wagon and rode it straight up a runaway truck ramp. When the smokey was taking information, didn't both drivers' licenses say John T. Baskin? Another driver lost his watch somewhere in Oklahoma, best he could figure, and two years later was running oranges and grapefruits, and found it stuck between the frame and the cross member of the bed he was pulling. It gets worse. A friend of mine was driving in the middle of the night and saw something dead on the road, thought it was a deer. Do you know, when he went back to see for himself, it was his brother that'd been hit."

"Get out."

Bobby held up his hand like he was taking an oath. "That's the God's honest truth. It gets stranger than that! They say there's a she-male somewhere in the Bayou. Heard about it for years, but I ain't never seen it."

"A man that dresses like a girl?" I asked with interest.

"No, not a queer. A half-and-half. What they called?" he asked a trucker on the stool next to us.

"'Maphrodite."

"That's right. What they say is it has sex for food, booze, money, even just a place to sleep. Heard from another trucker he thought he was getting a piece of ass, off come the pants, and this thing's got a dick and a pussy. He said he didn't know if he was supposed to suck or eat. I'll tell you, Danny, you stay at it long enough, you're liable to see just about everything there is to see."

His stories were meant to shock me, scare me into a better life.

But Bobby didn't know me back then. He didn't know that I had not only struggled through school but had also struggled through the concept of life. I had spent the better part of my youth standing back, void of understanding and feelings, watching other kids find and enjoy the basic pleasantries that would carry them to better things. Then, despite my mother's and guidance counselor's protests, I signed up for shop and automotives in high school. The only girl. It would take away my femininity, my mother cried. Maybe it would, but the first time I put my hands under the hood of a car, I went limp with pleasure. It felt right.

Once I was out of high school, I found that no one would hire me. I was a girl who was a mechanic, not a mechanic who happened to be a girl. After a very brief, oppressing experience working at an automotive shop, I got a job at a grocery store, and worked on cars for my parents' friends at night, in a garage my father rented for storage.

I didn't loathe my grocery job, but I didn't love it, either. Still, I would have stayed ringing up groceries until the end of time if it hadn't been for the clock-faced woman I waited on one snowy November night. The woman was scratching lottery tickets with her thumb nail while her groceries traveled slowly toward me on the conveyer belt like lazy passengers in an airport.

"I knew it. I just knew it!" she exclaimed. "And I didn't even need groceries."

Having already stuffed four bags full, I felt my eyebrows rise.

"It's this," she said, holding up her right palm. "It never lets me down. As soon as it starts to itch, I find the closest store. Looky here, ten on this one, free ticket on this, five on this…"

"That's some luck all right," I agreed.

She handed me the tickets and studied me. I tried to step back from her gaze, but I was trapped in my station. Her frame was oddly tiny, disproportional to her rotundness, her face too flat to be functional. Except for her nose, which was like a gnomon on a sundial, the rest of her face was level and spotted with moles. If it hadn't been evening, I would have dragged her outside to see if she could measure time.

"Not luck," she said. "Fate. Those tickets were meant for me."

"Well, it's good news whether it's luck or fate," I said.

She had to agree.

"You always seem to be looking for something," she said as she watched me stack her remaining items.

I usually recognized the regulars—this was a small family-owned operation—but nothing about her seemed familiar; God knows I wouldn't have forgotten that face.

"The way you stack the groceries, I mean. You stack and restack as if you were trying to predict your future. Some people use tea leaves, or tarot cards, or chicken bones, but you do it with groceries."

I studied the pile of items. The box of drier sheets I placed off to the side. A children's activity book of word circles and mazes, a tabloid magazine, and a children's-sized scrapbook were stacked on top of a carton of eggs. A lined notebook was last. I didn't see any revealing patterns.

Unexpectedly, she took hold of one of my hands, and, surprised, I tried to yank it back. She held tight, surely sensing I was embarrassed by the coarseness of it, the oil stains under the nails.

"Oh dear," she said, running her finger down my palm. "Do you want me to tell you?"

"No, ma'am," I said, thoroughly spooked.

"How about with this?" she asked, touching the pile.

Now I laughed a little and said, "All right, if you think you can."

"Drier sheets, comforts of home." She lifted the box and placed it softly on the belt away from the rest. "An empty notebook, your immediate future to fill in as you go. Activity book, chaos, confusion," she said, holding up the book of games. Then she took the tabloid magazine. "Oh dear, I get mixed feelings from this. They blend together and fall apart like they're dancing. Binge, spree, carnival, but I feel you running, still running. From? To, maybe? I don't know."

"And the scrapbook and eggs?" I asked, trying to bring her back, trying to sound as humored as I should have felt.

"Acceptance. Hope."

She paid for the groceries, taking everything but the notebook.

"Fill it," she said, handing it to me, before walking away.

She didn't give me a time frame, so I didn't know if she meant now or in the future. But one month later, using my notebook as an unofficial logbook, I sat behind the steering wheel of an eighteen-wheeler, relearning everything my father had once taught me when I was a child.

My very first night as a driver, in Charlotte, North Carolina, Bobby showed me which truck was his, and told me to ease mine into the line of sleeping rigs, right behind his. Another truck butted up close to mine, as though snuggling, keeping her safe from thieves. I crawled through the window situated between the seats of the cab into the sleeper box, and settled in. My new home was no bigger than a casket, with a reading light and a small vent in the side door, but it was the safest I'd ever felt. I slept solidly as if it were the first time in my life.

❧

Now, after so many years of spending nights in the sleeper, after experiencing more of Bobby's bizarre coincidentals than any one person should have to, I carry out a routine that I make myself believe gives me control over my thoughts, and the haunting dreams that are certain to follow.

I sit in the driver's seat and smoke my last cigarette, sucking on it slowly, letting the smoke fill my lungs to capacity, feeling it sail through my veins and out through the pores only to rest, like a shield, on my skin until I awaken from the peril that awaits me every night. After the second drag, I drop the visor and look at a photograph of Jesse. It's one of two. The other is in the sleeper box, taped to the back wall next to verses of a poem Jesse taught me to love, even memorize. It's the only time, now, we sleep face to face. Jesse Reid, a picture of imperfect perfection. The photo on the visor shows all of Jesse, and nothing at all. The sturdy right arm draped across the bar, the wide leather watch band around the thin wrist, a beer barely visible behind it, the coarse hand with a cigarette pinched between index finger and thumb. The left arm, the one that had once curled affectionately around my waist, rests modestly on the left thigh. The left leg is crossed placidly over the right thigh, the foot hiding behind the other calf, as though it doesn't want to be noticed, and the other firmly planted on the dirty floor, in front of the bar stool, the round-toed motorcycle boot pointing out ready for any surprises. The photo always makes me smile and feel sad at the same time.

After the cigarette, my one luxurious vice, I turn up the visor and let my thoughts drift to Dennis. He's always with me, but like a medium, haunted by strangers' spirits, I've taught myself how to block him out, how to keep him from trespassing in my personal space, at least while I'm awake. But Dennis, while not smart, is clever. He's delegated some of his power to those who sit on the side of thruways and interstates, alerting me of their presence as I drive by. Over time, most people disregard their wooden proxies, even those with photographs memorializing their lives. But not me; it's impossible. I see them as clearly as I see the trees, the guardrails, and the solid yellow lines. For me, some stand at attention, as if to salute my passing, while others want to be noticed, wailing, howling, or even going so far as to show me how it happened. If they're looking for someone to represent them, they've chosen the wrong person. When I figure out how, I'll ignore them the way I have Dennis.

Dennis still has moments of genius; he's as versatile as a spider, and manages, occasionally, to find a secret passage into my daydreams. I can't live without him any more than I can live without Jesse. Two halves of a whole. It makes me shudder.

After my last cigarette, I slide through the window into the sleeper, usually keeping my clothes and boots on in case I need to make a quick exit. I turn on my right side, and stare at the other picture of Jesse, pasted to the cushioned vinyl siding at eye level. I touch it, once, twice, maybe even a third time, and will myself to dream of happier times we had together.

But peculiar things happen when my eyes close, I'd like to think peculiar for everyone. You give into the darker side of yourself. It's like picking up a hitchhiker and passing over the keys. The body becomes a time machine, and the conscience is snuffed out as though with chloroform. The *I* is forced to give into the *you*, it's easier, it's safer. I want to dream about Jesse, but the *you* makes me dream about Dennis.

You always begin at the same time, in the same spot, thinking about the choices that put you where you are. You had four good years trucking before Bobby saw the black dog, and your parents were killed by a long-haul driver. That's when you quit and found work with the county. You tell yourself that it's a steadier job, decent money, and good benefits. And suddenly you blink your eyes and realize that three and a half years have gone by. You've tolerated it, until now.

You've jumped off your roller a thousand times, but today is different.

You've landed in the space between the roller and the gang truck. You know there are tools and people and trucks around you, but you notice only Dennis standing on the road beside your machine. He flips you off. You think to yourself, *If I wouldn't get fired, I'd punch his lights out.* He peers at you with a hint of humor, like he's heard you, like he thinks you're too cowardly to do such a thing. Dismissing you with a wave, he does something he's not supposed to do, and climbs onto your machine. Time stops like it did then; there's a breeze and even though you're sweating in your dream, in real life you pull the sheet up to your chin and curl your legs to your chest for warmth.

You'll deal with him in a minute, and you continue forward, toward a machine you think has broken down, but then something stops you, the sound of the back-up beeper coming from your roller. The back-up beeper echoes in your dream and you tell yourself, *If I don't wake up, I'm going to go deaf.* But in the dream, you don't care what it sounds like, you care that it's sounding. You stop and turn to look and see Dennis flip you off again before turning to look behind him. You say to him, "You're a stupid bastard." But nobody on earth can hear over that goddamned back-up beeper. You put your hands over your ears, you open your mouth to scream, but you see that Dennis has beaten you to it. He screams and screams, but no one can hear it because of the beeper. Somehow you hear it with perfect clarity. His screams have grabbed hold of your eardrums and run with them. There is nothing in the world that's important enough to be heard over his screams. He wants your undivided attention, and he's made sure he's gotten it.

You run toward him, toward the roller, toward what is about to become a disaster, toward the thing that's going to change your life forever. Your mouth opens to warn him, but you can't hear the noise you're making and neither can he.

yellow journalism
a flamboyant and irresponsible approach to news reporting

The Journal, Friday, August 11, 1995
"Worker Killed Wasn't Machine's Driver"
By Ron Taft, staff writer

A county worker was killed early this morning when an eighteen-thousand-pound roller pinned him to the ground. Dennis Lutz, thirty-eight, of 292 Parker Lane, was trapped when he tried to jump free of the machine. The road crew was working on Bishop Road in southern Jacob County.

The roller slid down a two-foot embankment and landed on its right side. Three-quarters of Lutz's body was pinned beneath the machine, said Deputy David Spur. Lutz was rushed to St. Michael's Memorial Hospital where he was pronounced dead on arrival. The Department of Labor is investigating.

"When the chipper breaks down, everything stops. Maybe Denny thought he was helping. For some reason he backed the roller up," said a co-worker. But according to summer aide Donna Abbott, tension was brewing on the oiling crew. "Dennis didn't get along with our foreman, Danny Fletcher. It seemed like he was waiting for an opportunity to get her into trouble. Dennis didn't think a woman should run a crew. He said so all the time." Other workers interviewed said tension is a part of any job that has a time schedule to meet. When questioned by reporters, Danny Fletcher said, "There was a lot of traffic, not just DOT, but regular traffic. All our trucks were heading south, right past us. There was so much noise he just couldn't hear me when I called for him to stop the machine. Everyone is shaken by this. I lectured the crew about safety at the beginning of the summer. I do every year. Accidents like this shouldn't happen."

displaced

to remove from the usual or proper place

I'm highballing down I95, sitting on a 600-horsepower engine and a 10-speed transmission, with steel rods shaped like arrows on the bed behind me. If I stop short, they'll spear my intestines. I drive faster, aiming; I'm a bullet astray of its trajectory, searching for the mark.

I can't stop laughing; my bones rattle against each other. I feel the way I do when I've tried to quit smoking. I'll go the whole day without a single cigarette, and then find myself hunched in the dark, against the garage door, hiding from myself and the eyes of people who watch me, dragging on a cigarette as if it's the last breath I'll ever take.

It's December, and I've been driving again almost two months, only this time in my own truck. I've done thirty runs, hauling everything from gun barrels to insulation board, from onions to cow hides. I've traveled from Boston to Miami, from Bangor to Seattle, putting in four hundred and eighty hours and nearly 22,000 miles. I've walked away from a decent job with the county, from Buzz and Deena, from Agnes and Horace. Their eyes are still on me, even after two months. If I stop short, they'll puncture my soul. As time ticks by it becomes alarmingly clear there are eyes on me wherever I go. Day, night, rain, shine, someone is always watching me. I ride hard and fast, trying to keep out of their sight.

I'm so alert I border on manic. I feel like I've been turned inside out. My nerve endings are like live wires arcing unrestrained after a storm. Every time a large bug hits my windshield, I'm nearly startled out of my skin. I drive faster, into the night. Yellow becomes blue becomes orange becomes brown becomes black becomes charcoal…and I wait to see the black dog. This is the time of night he comes out, I'm sure of it, as charcoal becomes gray becomes green becomes blue becomes yellow. Dexedrine and methedrine are useless to me, though I sweat as heavily as an addict and smell just as bad too. I am my own drug. Not even a little tired, I've had to stop for fuel, for the toilet, for brew and donuts. I eat four. I eat a jar of peanuts and three super-sized Slim Jims, drink two sodas and two bottles of water. Still, I lose weight. My stomach sinks, tucks, stretches around my rib cage like a fitted sheet.

I pull into a rest area and climb back to the sleeper. It's an empty home, no more than eight feet long and forty-two feet wide, with diamond-shaped vinyl patterns, wall-papered with the few articles written about Dennis. The last is dated October 7, three days before I left the county. I haven't taped up pictures of my parents or Bobby. I'm plagued enough by the dead without looking at them too. My boots weigh my feet down like anchors. The rest of me follows like slack rope, so I quickly untie then pop them off. I close my eyes but I'm suddenly hot. The heat is poking through the windows, and I feel like I'm being cooked by a 100-watt bulb in an Easy Bake oven. I strip off my jeans, socks, underwear, T-shirt, and sports bra. I even take off my necklace with the cross, before putting it back on. I'm not religious but it's something Bobby's wife wanted me to have.

I lie down and study myself from this angle. One of my lovers was skinny and long, like me. We were close; I enjoyed his company, his laugh. The sex was good. He had a few flaws, though. He talked too much. And his hands were too thick, too large, too much like Ping-Pong paddles. The worst was his name, Tracey. Everything was good between us, until he told me he loved me, then asked me to marry him. I had to leave him. He was a nice guy, but he was too skinny to carry my burdens along with his own.

I look down the length of my body and try to remember the last time I had sex. At first, I think it was a long time ago with Tracey, but then I remember the romp with my co-worker, Pip, before I left.

Cupping my hands over my breasts I think, of all people, about Buzz, my closest friend from the county. Our best conversations were in our plow as we waited for the snow to fall. Because of our infatuation with breasts, we talked about them a lot. With anyone else the conversation would have been sexual harassment, but Buzz was like a brother to me. Once in a while I had a feeling he reflected upon a different kind of relationship even though he was married to Deena. The birthday cards and small thoughtful gifts, but then I knew Deena did the shopping.

His wife had large breasts, huge double-Ds.

You're lucky, I told him. Guys love big boobs. Now take me, for instance. Most men are disappointed when they finally get a look at these suckers. Technically, in the land of lingerie, I don't need a bra. They make 'em this size because they feel sorry for us. We're kinda like the bench warmers on a sports team, wearing the jersey so we look like we belong.

Speed bumps, Buzz said. There are two kinds. Perky ones trip you up, put dents in your rims if you go over too fast. They're irritating wannabes. The others are the slopes. They're there as reminders: go slow, move over me gently. That's what you've got.

I pulled my sweatshirt from my neck and looked down. I can handle slopes.

I cover my slopes with the palm of my hands and will sleep to come. Car doors slam, engines rev, some trucks downshift, others hiss the air brakes. People talk, dogs bark, babies cry. Why the hell is everything accentuated? Dennis and his death and his house with all the clocks and his life have cursed me.

I'm up and dressed and jump out of my truck, jiggling Greek worry beads Bobby's wife gave me. They're small and gold, easy to handle, quick to calm me, just like Bobby was. I go to the bathroom, get another thermos of brew, two packages of Rolos, a bag of sunflower seeds, gum, and a carton of cigarettes, and drop all of it on the counter. The clerk rings me up and I pull my wallet out of my back pocket.

The woman behind me yanks her child against her, as if I've

drawn a gun. She's looking at the chain that binds my wallet to my jeans. "There's lots of villainy out there," I say and smile at her and the kid. The kid smiles back. He likes my wallet on a chain. The truth is, sitting on a wallet for hours at a time is bad for the back. This way, when I pull it out in the truck, it's still attached and I can't lose it. But what does she care? Now the husband comes up and looks me over. He gives this disgusted snort, like I've just had the nerve to step into the Queen Mother's private quarters. I walk away from them, toward the exit. Forty feet away, something makes me stop and turn. He's leaning toward his wife, I watch his mouth move, and he says to her, "That's what they call a Diesel Dyke." She smiles.

If I heard it from this distance, then everyone must have heard it. I look around to see who's looking at me, but no one seems to have noticed. He sees me looking at him, shakes his head and stares at me hard, his mouth closed in a straight, critical line. My teachers used to look at me like that. As he stares, in his mind he says, *All she needs is a good screw.* I hightail it out of there and go to my truck, wiping my brow with my forearm. When I see him come out of the building and walk toward his car, my legs move me until I stop in front of him.

"I heard that," I threaten.

"Heard what?"

Good question. Technically, his mouth didn't move.

"I heard you," I say again, slowly. "You have no right to judge me. You don't know me."

"I don't need to judge your actions," he says. "God will."

I take a couple steps backward, so enraged I'm afraid I might grab him around the neck and choke him to death. Instead, I say, "When it's your turn he's gonna say, 'This guy sure was an experiment gone wrong.'"

I don't know why I got so angry. I should be used to being judged. Women like me working jobs like this must be lesbians; I've heard it a thousand times over. The majority of the county men I worked with thought I was, and I gave them no reason to believe otherwise. Tracey meant a lot to me, but he was a part of my life that had nothing to do with DOT or trucks. We never went to the same bars, restaurants, or parties that my co-workers went to. I kept Tracey to myself. The only ones I shared him with were Buzz and Deena. Once a month the four of us got together. They honored my wishes and kept my private life private.

After the steel rods have been delivered in Charleston, I head north with a load of watermelons that need to be delivered immediately to Hunts Point Market, New York City. I'm barreling up I95 when my front rear end explodes. I coast to a stop and have to walk off the interstate to find a phone. After calling my dispatcher and a tow truck, I walk back to my truck to wait. I don't want it to end up in a chop shop. This might be bad luck, but at least it didn't happen in Hunts Point Market. Once, I saw a driver get robbed of his load there. Most drivers won't go into the city at night because of the danger; instead, they wait till morning and go in with the rest of the commuters. As far as I'm concerned, though, there's no choice, the load is expected to be delivered at a certain time. If we wait, too much time and money is lost.

The damage to my truck is disabling. By the time a new truck picks up the load, and mine is in tow, it's nearly nine-thirty at night. The tow-truck driver drops me off at the pay phone I already used and I walk a block down the road toward a bar called the Yellow Submarine. It advertises drink specials, food, and rooms, but says nothing about continental breakfasts or HBO.

Every parking spot is filled with run-down cars and pickups, or pickmeups, as drivers call them. There are even a few big trucks parked parallel to the road. I study them, hoping it's someone I know, but I don't recognize any. Snuggled along the wall, hidden in darkness, is a customized Harley-Davidson Panhead. Up close, the chrome shines in the night. This bike has a reason to be proud of itself. Its appearance is spectacular. I run my hand up and over the "sissy bar" and exhale slowly. I'm delirious with envy.

Inside, the bar seems like all the others on the road, but here, I sense something is different.

The smell of stale beer isn't as distinctive, though it borders the premises like an electric fence. There's another smell I can't place. It catches my nose, drifts, then evaporates.

It's not a shabby bar, rather clean compared to most I've been in, but I can't shake the feeling that it's still a trucker bar, and most have a dark side to them, like the slightest disturbance will raise something from its slumber. The decor is a mix between ocean paraphernalia—photographs of beaches and sunsets—and the Beatles. Behind the bar is the usual display of liquor and beer bottles, but mixed in is a trumpet, an old guitar hanging from the wall, and a harmonica. Cut into the bar is an ocean buoy with the warning bell still intact.

When you first walk in, the bar is on the left. That's also where one dartboard is. The rest is tables and chairs and dance floor. Past the dance floor there are two pool tables, more dartboards, Ms. Pac-Man and Centipede games, and a pinball machine. Down the hall is the entrance to the motel.

I look around me doubtfully, then move to a bar stool and wait. Southerners are the slowest creatures on earth. The bartender appears to be one of the men playing darts. He calls that he'll be with me in a second. In southern time, a second lasts anywhere from five to twenty minutes. He's back behind the bar in ten.

"What'll it be?" he asks, placing a napkin in front of me.

"How about something dark," I say.

"Ma'am?" he questions, politely drawing attention to the fact that I'm older than him.

"Dark beer," I clarify.

"Draft." It isn't a question.

"Bottle," I insist.

He smiles to himself. He's a tall man of twenty-three maybe. The makings of his mustache look as though he's glued straw to his upper lip. His face is pockmarked, and he wears big square tinted glasses. He hasn't moved to get my beer.

"Where you from, Yankee?" he asks kindly, his voice high pitched and nasally.

"New York."

"I always wanted to see Lady Liberty."

"I'm from way upstate. Not downstate."

"New Yorkers are New Yorkers," he says.

"You've obviously never been locked in a room with a downstater."

He shrugs, doesn't get it. Two customers are waiting to order and I tap my empty napkin, then point down to them. Instead of waiting on them, he leans down and says, "You look like you're looking for somethin'. Are you hungry?"

"I could eat."

He places a stained paper menu in front of me and taps it. "Look this over."

"Should I expect you back tonight?" I ask.

He laughs and wags a finger at me.

He returns—still without my beer—to take my order, then I turn on the bar stool and look around. The Beatles are on the walls, on the juke box, even free standing in a corner. I wonder if, like Elvis, we'll have a sighting. Even down the hallway to the bathrooms, at the back of the bar, photos, posters, 45s, and album covers blanket the walls. I'm curious now, and I make my way down the hall. I'm impressed. This is a Christie's auction begging to be discovered.

There's a closed door at the end of the hall. As I walk toward it, the smell I can't place becomes more potent, though I still can't quite put my finger on it. Behind the door the bass of John Lennon's "Come Together" beckons me like a finger. The door is cheap lauan that I could punch my hand through. The lock has been broken, so I don't feel like I'm actually trespassing. When I cross the threshold, I feel as if I've stepped into the song. The entrance before me is as dark, as murky, and as suggestive as the strange lyrics.

Then I know the smell. It's the smell of sex. I follow it like a dog sniffing out food.

Straight ahead there are six doors from which I can choose. I should feel embarrassed by my voyeurism, but I'm breathing as heavily as any one of the women behind the closed doors. I press my hand against one door frame, slowly gripping the tarnished knob in my other. I turn and press at the same time, urging the door open as though I already know it will stick at the top.

Peering through the small crack, I watch a trucker I've seen on past runs going at it with a woman. She seems to be enjoying it. I'm surprised that a hooker is that enthusiastic; I thought it went against their code of ethics. I feel myself actually gearing up to cheer him on, and have to cover my mouth to keep myself quiet. My nerves are already jittery as I back away from the door, shocked by my behavior, how I feel. And then I hear, "Can I help you find something?"

A startled yelp escapes my lips, and I fall against the wall behind me, my hand on my chest, over my heart.

"Jesus," I mumble. "You scared the hell out of me."

The person staring at me from across the hall leans against the corner, arms folded securely across the chest.

"Are you lost?" The question is actually an accusation.

I'm still trying to catch my breath, so the lie snags in my throat. "I was looking for the bathroom."

"You mean the bathroom back there, the one you passed in order to get here?" The person jabs a thumb backward and then a finger at the ground.

I'm caught, we both know it, but my accuser isn't giving me a way out. I shift uncomfortably and then shuffle back the way I came. I'm unsure whether the person standing by the doorway is male or female. The red exit sign and a dirty light bulb dangling from the ceiling are all I have to work with. The voice is a soft southern tenor, too high to be male, too low to be female. As I approach, I see that the hair is almond brown, parted on the right side and slicked back in the old James Dean style. The hair line around the side burns—which leads me to believe male— remind me of a coast line, a mix between Italy and Florida. The body is very slim, an inch or two taller than me. I try to take it all in without being obvious. A white T-shirt under a flannel shirt. Blue jeans. Black round-toe biker boots. All my type. If this is a man, I'm in trouble. I'm about to fly in ecstasy.

I try to squeeze through the doorway but my new acquaintance won't move out of the way. I notice a few whiskers on the chin and am instantly elated. This could be lust at first sight. I can see myself getting to know him by way of CB and then falling onto a mattress—after two long months of mutual airwave masturbation—with such a yearning in my loins, that I'll begin eating before the wrappers come off.

Alex, who was before Tracey, was like that. But it wasn't about impatience alone, it was about fear and loss, and even permanence too. After a couple weeks together, he wanted to own two recliners with our ass marks already worn into them. You're moving too fast, I told him. But I love you, he said. Well, you can't love me, I said to him…I said to all of them. But I do. Lame excuse, and I was gone.

As I contemplate my former lover, this possibility still hasn't moved, and in order to get by I'm going to have to push my way through.

"You shouldn't judge," he says.

I want to laugh. Me, judge?

"You're assuming she's a hooker, isn't that right? Yet you don't know their circumstances. They could be married; he may have just come off the road. They may be dating. He may have found out he's dying, and this is one of the last times he'll ever have sex again. This could even be a honeymoon."

I hold my hands up to say, *Back off, I'm not judging*, but deep down, I am. I'm shocked that she would go to bed with a man she doesn't know, even as I stand here contemplating doing the same thing with this man. But I tell myself that she's the one who sits at the end of every bar in every small town, USA, checking out every trucker who walks through the door, knowing she'll take any one of them to bed, no matter what their age, or looks, or marital status.

He watches me as these thoughts cross my mind. Then, as though he's in my head and has heard them, he gives me a questioning, accusing glare. *Are you any different?* his stare asks.

No, asshole. Thanks for pointing it out.

"Gary wants me to tell you that your supper is getting cold." *Suppa* is how he pronounces it.

He waves me ahead, and I have no choice but to pass in front of him. A woman in heels and a skirt would take the opportunity and swing her hips. But that's hard to do when the back pocket of your jeans is ripped and a pair of plaid boxers is hanging out.

My dinner and a plastic cup filled with a pee-yellow substance sit on the bar top.

"I asked for something dark," I say to Gary, who's playing darts again.

The man from the hallway sits two stools down from me, in a spot by the wall that looks like it's been his since the dawn of man. A glass of beer, a bowl of pretzels, a paper weight on top of a yellow tablet, two packs of Camels, and a black ashtray surround him like Christmas presents. Gary is ignoring me, and my new friend is smiling at my dissatisfaction.

"I asked for a bottle of something dark," I direct it at him this time.

"This is the south, darlin'. You get what you get."

"And just what the hell is this?" I ask, pointing to my food.

"That is called southern delight. It's what you ordered from the menu. You've got your delicious boiled okra, surely you recognize corn, a nice heavy sausage gravy over biscuits, and a breaded hog jowl."

I push the plate and cup away.

"You're awful sassy for a Yankee in southern territory."

"Look," I growl at him. "Is there a restaurant and a hotel around here?"

"You're settin' in one."

Now I stare hard.

"Oh, you mean something a bit more respectable? If you

jump back on the interstate and go north a couple exits, you just might find a place that's suitable for you."

I breathe heavily. "My truck broke down."

"Pity," he says and lights a cigarette.

"Can you at least tell me where the cigarette machine is?"

"Broke," he says and drags deeply on his to tease me. "Why is it that you northerners haven't learned yet how to graciously accept our southern hospitality?"

"Tell me, do they make Southern Comfort in your primitive land? Or do I need to travel six hundred miles north, to a more civilized area, in order to get something decent to drink?"

Gary now looks over at us, and hollers, "Jesse, would you mind getting our friend a drink?"

"I'm fixin' to," he says but takes a couple more drags off his cigarette before he moves.

Jesse goes behind the bar and looks around as if he's never been back there before. There's a line of shot glasses in front of me, so I pick one up and hand it to him. One side of his mouth is up in a smirk. He's looking down at the glass in his hand, pouring the shot slowly. Then holds another shot glass up and says, "You are going to buy me a shot for waiting on you like this, aren't you?"

He holds his glass up for me to clink, which I'm obligated to do, and watches me gulp. He's leaning down on his forearms, that smirk now spread across his whole face. He reaches below him and pulls out a bowl, and pushes it with two fingers toward me.

"These here are baked goods that southerners call pretzels. Are they good enough for your sensitive palate?"

"I'd do better with a cigarette," I say, but eat a pretzel anyway since I'm starving.

He goes back to his seat and shakes the pack at me. A cigarette pops up like a piece of toast. I reach for it and notice that Jesse has yet to take his eyes off me or to drink his shot. I decide to give him a dose of his own medicine, but something stops me and I try to break it down. He's clean, his clothes aren't old, his boots are Harley, his demeanor standoffish. Then it occurs to me, I don't think I've ever met anyone as pretty. His eyelashes are long and curled and black. His eyes are not only almond colored, like his hair, but almond shaped. His lips are nearly heart shaped, as perfectly outlined and red as a woman who uses outlining pencil. He's watching me watch him, acts suddenly self-conscious, fumbles with the cigarette pack, and looks away, embarrassed.

I search my pockets for my lighter, but it's in the truck with my cigarettes. Jesse sees me digging and pulls out a square silver lighter. I reach for it, but he pulls his hand back and opens it, running his thumb down the flint. The flame is small, it lights up his eyes and eyebrows. I'm watching him again, because he is so nice to look at. He clears his throat and looks down.

"I guess you're in need of a room."

I nod reluctantly.

"Gary," Jesse calls. "Our friend here needs a room. You got anything available?"

Gary puts his darts down and reaches for a book behind the bar.

"Well, technically no." Gary studies Jesse, Jesse studies Gary, and they have a silent conversation.

After a minute or so Jesse nods and says, "You want me to show, well, what's your name, darlin'?"

I sigh. I hate this part. "Danny," I mumble.

They both stare at me as if I'm kidding, and I lift my shoulders to show I'm not.

"All right. You want me to show Danny where her room is?"

"I guess, but she didn't eat her supper. Something wrong with it?"

"It's been a long day," I say. "I'm too tired to eat."

He nods, like it's an acceptable excuse. Then he says to Jesse, "She's going to miss the ten-thirty show."

"I don't know that Danny is up for that kind of fun. You know how uptight northerners are."

"You can give me the key and I'll find the room myself."

"Maybe she'll visit our fine establishment another time and stay for the entertainment," Jesse says to Gary, as though I haven't spoken.

Then Jesse asks if I have a bag, which I do, tucked under the bar, and he carries it through the Employees Only door, closing it behind us. He turns left and pulls a key out of his pocket, and unlocks a door. There are three rooms, one on the left and two on the right. Mine is the first on the right. He flicks the light on and places the bag on the bed. I survey the room and turn toward the window. A faceless image reflects from behind my shoulder, into the dark glass, and I jump back a step. I know I'm not safe from them on the road, but now here too?

"You scared of your own reflection?" I'm not obliged to answer so he says, "You're awful jumpy, but then northerners generally are."

I'm breathing heavy. I want to laugh because I want to cry. Madness taps me on the shoulder every time I turn my back on it. I decide that if I keep going like this, I could slip away without anyone knowing.

I look around the room. "I don't belong here," I say and reach for my bag.

He takes it from me and says, "Y'all just need some sleep. You'll feel better in the mornin'."

As if he's read my fear, he goes over to the window and closes the curtain, then walks past me and goes through the door across the hall. He's in there for a few minutes before coming back with two shot glasses, a bottle of Jack Daniels, a dark brown beer bottle, two bananas, and a chocolate bar. Now I really do want to weep. He pours the two shots, then the dark beer into a small glass from the bathroom. He even peels a banana. "We can't have you wasting away in the middle of the night. You have a bill to pay in the mornin'."

I accept everything he offers and sit next to him on the bed. He flinches when my arm rubs his, then gets up and makes a production about retrieving his cigarettes from the small round table by the window. He pours two more shots and lights two cigarettes, hands one of each to me but goes back to the table. I'm disappointed. I can't hide it.

And I can't stand the silence another minute so I say, "You have a room here?"

He nods and points across the hall.

"Are you a driver? I don't recall seeing you on any runs this way."

"No, I live here."

"In town?"

"Nope, I live here." He points to the ground.

"In the bar?"

"That's right. That room right there is my home."

It seems odd, but I don't say so.

Then we're silent but Jesse watches every move I make. I study my arm, pick at a scab. After a full cigarette of silence, I say, "You're not much of a conversationalist."

"You're doin' fine on your own."

"And you left your sense of humor across the hall?"

Jesse raises an eyebrow and doesn't crack a smile.

"Do you work?"

"I help Gary on occasion."

"Do you work outside of that?"

"No."

"Are you a native of South Carolina?"

"No." I have to put my hands out so he'll go on. "Alabama."

"That's why you sound different."

"Is that a question or a statement?"

"You haven't asked where I'm from."

"I already know you're from New York, upstate, that is, not to be mistaken with downstate."

"Is there anything else you'd like to know?"

"I've heard about you," Jesse says. "There aren't many lady drivers out there." I'm staring at him as though he's just revealed some big secret about me. He sees that I'm uncomfortable so he adds, "You weren't the only one who knew Bobby. He mentioned you now and again."

I stand, go for a cigarette. I still can't talk about Bobby. He was all I had in the trucking world, and when I lost him, I lost my hunger, and most of my direction. I keep my back to Jesse, and I know he senses that Bobby is not a subject I intend to talk about.

He says, "It's late. Get some rest. You're safe here. You can go through the hall door, it locks from the other side, no one can get in from the other way."

Out of his shirt pocket he pulls two keys, a sealed pack of cigarettes, and a folded piece of paper, and places them on the table.

"Are you turning in too?" I ask, hopeful even though he hasn't shown an interest.

Jesse pulls a pocket watch out of his right pocket and says, "They're expecting me out there. Sure you don't want to come?"

I shake my head and say, "But thanks for all this."

He nods and steps out of the room.

"Jesse," I call.

He opens the door and pokes his head in.

"What's your last name?"

"James," he says before closing the door lightly.

I think about that for a few seconds before going to the table and tearing open the cigarettes. He's left his silver lighter and I light a cigarette before unfolding the paper. On it is written Jesse Reid. I laugh a little. He's also written the name, address, and phone number of the bar, and the phone number to his room. Under that he's written:

If you need anything, Danny Fletcher, you come across and get me. I'm nocturnal so you won't be disturbing me one bit. We're glad to finally have you here.

altered state
conventional time loses meaning; one is caught in extradimensional adventures

I went back on the road on October 10, exactly two months after Dennis's death. It was painful knowing Bobby wasn't out there at a truck stop waiting for me, but the loneliness I felt in my old life was worse. Yes, I missed the Tuesday night bowling with Buzz and Deena, the Friday night dollar drafts and ten-cent wings. During the winter Buzz and I spent just about every night plowing, so I wasn't bored. But in that life, something was missing, and my heart ached.

The people who were closest to me, the ones who knew me during good and bad times, were gone. My one real friend was really only mine seasonally. Buzz still couldn't understand that even though as a friend I could tell him anything, I wanted a lover who I didn't have to tell anything to. The life I made for myself living in Central New York as a county worker, though, was a different kind of loneliness. I went to the same house every night, ate the same quick-fix meals, stared at the same four walls. Like a cancer, it consumed me from the inside out. On the road, loneliness was easier to live with because most truckers are loners. That kind of lonely I felt on the open road was different. On the road, choices were mine. I didn't have a boss to tell me how and when and where and why. I could sit in a bar and talk to any person who showed an interest in me. Any kind of companionship would do. The silence I lived with all day long was enough to swallow me whole, but it was a silence that I chose.

Buzz tried to teach me not to take life so seriously. By the end of winter—hell by the third serious snowfall—drivers either hated us because we and our saltshakers hadn't gotten the snow plowed and the salt down fast enough, or they hated us because we and our saltshakers drove too slow and they couldn't get around us without getting sprayed and losing control of their cars.

Spring slowed down for us, we could go two weeks without a single flake before the last storm that was hiding in Canada or Michigan came rushing in when our backs were turned. It's the same thing every year. And Central New Yorkers were forgetters. They forgot how immobilized life was with snow on the ground. We suddenly became heroes again, jumping out of our phone booths to save the day. Buzz was there to remind me not to take it too personally. He was a good companion.

Things happen to you when you work for the county for too long. The mind warps and you dream about frying an egg on the hot steamy tar that has just been poured down on the road in front of you. Every day is as murky, grim, and dirty as the day before; every day is as monotonous and dull as the men you sit with five, six, sometimes seven days a week in greasy diners and oily trucks. What else is there to do but tell, retell, and revise your life story, a story that eventually becomes as boring to you as it is to them.

After the thousandth "I remember when…" a series of realities hit, the first like a sledgehammer in the chest, with the rest falling like dominoes: you're a county worker—a goddamn county worker, you realize. You made this choice, I told myself, to get away from all those thoughts, which started out as simple speculations but turned into obsessions. They were enough to drive me crazy. I calculated the number of miles it took me to get from here to there at seventy miles per hour, and how it would differ once I changed my route, my actual driving, my speed, calculating that diesel was $1.29 to the gallon, at a hundred-and-twenty-thousand gallons per year, my truck got six-and-a-half miles to the gallon. The more conservatively I drove, the less money I spent. By not powering as I went down the grade, I wouldn't burn any excess fuel and it also prevented the engine from lugging. Easy starts, progressive shifting, keeping the RPMs steady, no jack-rabbit starts or hotdogging, frequent tune ups. All this reduced costs by ten percent. In layman's terms, the less money I spent, the more I pocketed in the end.

I thought that if I changed my job, the thoughts would change too.

But the thoughts were still there. And I realized I was going nowhere, doing absolutely nothing with my life. I had no one to love and no one to love me back; my "I remember whens" were really someone else's or even worse, they were about work, not real life.

When I first left trucking, after my parents were killed, when I was trying to make myself feel positive about the change, I thought it'd be better when the college kids came for the summer. But I only felt that way my first summer on the job. Those fresh young faces, those virginal ears motivated me, gave me hope, gave me a reason to rethink my life and what I'd accomplished. Then the kids told their stories, and I realized they'd done more in three years of college than I only dreamed of doing in an entire lifetime. By the second week of that first summer on the job, I knew damn well that my "somedays" were loaded with bullshit. And I was angry. I took it out on the college kids. They thought the world revolved around them, and it did outside of the DOT, but not at the county. This job was their slap into reality: you're a goddamn county worker, kid. You see that guy over there—I pointed to a new full-timer who was feeling good about himself—he was once you. All your college education has gained you is an orange flag. You're not even good enough to drive the big yellow machine, like the Tonka trucks you used to push around with those soft little hands. In our world, you're nothing.

But it wasn't them who'd turned into nothings, it was me. And I didn't like myself one bit because of it.

After just two days back on the road, I felt like I'd never left. I'd missed it, really. The camaraderie, the greasy food, the banter.

That is, until I was stuck on I83, behind miles of traffic, the CB chattering like a nervous father-to-be.

"Hey, driver, what the hell's with all the brake lights?" I called into my mic.

"Couple a fuckin' four wheelers trying to outrun each other. You southbound, driver?"

"Roger. I'm just coming in the backdoor. Hope you don't mind, right," I said.

"What's it look like over your shoulder, I'm back out?" he replied.

"Saw an aerial plane awhile back when I was running solo. This accident'll keep 'em busy. Lots of four wheelers behind me."

"Where you headed, right?"

"The Big A, over," I answered, referring to Atlanta.

"I'll be home in bed with my better half before you ever get past this accident, right."

Another driver responded quickly, excitedly. "I'd know that sexy voice anywhere. Is that you, Danny, hidin' behind a new handle, back out?"

Two other truckers jumped into the conversation, and I was immediately smiling, forgetting for a few minutes that I had food to deliver. You're back, they kept saying. You've finally come back. You've been missed. Your face, your smile, your body. I been lookin' for a lady to get friendly with, one says. Sure wouldn't be no decent lady doin' what you want to do, I replied. Someone laughed and said, You're the prettiest trucker I've ever known. Well, there isn't much competition, I joked. The sexual innuendo and teasing back and forth gave me the motivation I'd needed. For a few seconds, I felt like a woman again. I'd been without sleep for twenty-four hours, yet I felt like I could carry my truck to its destination. When it was time to part I said, This is Archer and I'm back out.

I delivered my load and picked up a bed of lumber to be delivered to Louisiana.

Louisiana frightened me. I've always been superstitious and

am uncomfortable with the tales of voodoo and hexes. Anyone who worships snakes, the dead, spirits, and twins, has too much time on their hands. I delivered my load quickly, trying to shake the feeling of impending doom, fueled up and jumped on I10, then made plans to pick up a delivery in a day and a half in Tennessee. Even though I hadn't slept in nearly forty-eight hours, I didn't want to stop until I was out of Louisiana. The first exit in Mississippi would do.

It was dusk, but there wasn't much traffic, which I found strange. On the way down I had had eleven HOGs playing leapfrog. When it had gotten too windy one of them had come on the radio and asked if they could run with me. I found myself running front door for them. Another keyed in and told me I'd be amply rewarded before the day's end. I stopped at an eat 'em up, and they stopped with me. There were eleven men and eight women. Harley's through and through. I admired their tattoos and leather, showed them mine on my pelvic bone, the yang of the yin and yang principles that I got one drunken night after a month straight on the road. The tattoo artist passed out before he could finish the other half.

Back on the road again, day turned to early evening, and our split off was rapidly approaching. They'd be taking I75 while I'd continue toward Louisiana. I'd miss seeing the black glasses and helmets veer into the hammer lane every ten miles or so, miss hearing their stories. Their two-mile warning blazed green and, like birds, they crossed into the passing lane in the upside-down V formation. I wondered what it would be like to be the front door on a HOG.

The first biker approached and his female rider said, "You gonna be all right by yourself? You won't have anyone to keep you awake?"

"I'll manage," I said.

"How about we leave you with something to think about if you get tired?"

Each man gave a thumbs-up while each woman raised her shirt to give me a glimpse of her breasts. As to Cs zoomed by and I laughed, shaking my head, deciding I didn't want to hurt their feelings and let them know they misjudged me. Their going-away gift was a tender act. As the last Harley passed, I gave them three long shrieks from my horn, honks much more powerful than I give kids who drive by and signal.

I was glad they weren't with me now, though. The storm that was brewing in the Gulf had begun to crash New Orleans. From what I could make out, it had its eye on Biloxi and Mobile, Alabama too. Bluish-black clouds were cresting in the sky and I felt like I was driving through the middle of Moses's Red Sea, but he was nowhere to be found, already safe and sound on the other side. Which meant I was toast.

Just past Baton Rouge, thunder and lightning hit. It should've been behind me, but streaks of lightning ran vertically from sky to ground in front of me. The interstate was heavily wooded on both sides, darkening an already rapidly approaching night. I'd had a dream a couple nights before where something blacker than the dark crept across my wall, moving slowly, slowly, a silent intruder, the shadow of something bigger than everything good. I felt the same sense of being overcome when I noticed the rusty old Volkswagen Rabbit in front of me. It had come out of nowhere. But there it was, purposely slowing, an arm out the window, waving me past. I checked the spot mirror for cars, and seeing nothing, I crossed lanes and passed, then went back into the granny lane. The Rabbit passed me again and cut in front of me. I put on the brakes and backed off, but he anticipated and did the same thing. Once again, the arm came out indicating me to pass. I'd play this game once more. By the time I veered back into the right lane, he was already out and passing me. Fucking prick, I thought, gritting my teeth. I was tempted to haul the front end of my truck right up his ass—there was no one around to see—but I backed off. He waved and hit the accelerator. I guessed he must have been going eighty, eighty-five. Suddenly his car swerved, first left, then a quick right, overcorrecting, at which point it kicked up on the right tires, flipped onto the hood and skidded off the road, spun and flipped back on the tires. By the time I stopped I was a ways ahead of him, but I ran down the interstate toward the car anyway. There wasn't another car in sight. I was all he had.

As I approached, I noticed a small wooden cross wedged into the ground almost directly below the car. I reached the driver's side and the guy glanced out at me but the only thing he moved were his eyes. The metal piece that the headrest slid onto had gone into the back of his head and through his forehead. He waited for me to speak to him, but I bent forward and vomited. I went back to him, and he was still watching me.

I started to say, I'll call for the meat wagon, but quickly caught myself. "I'll call for help," I said, even though I was thinking, *There's no point.*

"That's all right, I'll wait," he said calmly, as if I'd just offered him a ride but he decided the bus would do fine.

"Everything will be all right. A quick stay at the hospital and you'll be home in no time," I tried to assure him. I could barely get myself to say it. I turned, ready to run to my truck but he said,

"No, this is fine. This is home now."

Clearly, he was delirious; there was a piece of metal through his head.

"Stay here," I said, then shook my head for saying something that stupid. I ran as hard as I could back to my truck. All at once the mic was in my hand, it was keyed, and I jumped out of the truck to take another look, but there was no car there. My heart was beating so hard and fast I let go of the mic and sat on the ground, staring. There was nothing there. I started to crawl toward the wreck that was no longer there, then pushed to my feet and ran. There was nothing there but the cross and old wilted flowers. I picked one up and it crumpled in my hand. I looked around frantically, as if the guy just plucked his head up and walked off. I ran to the tree line and looked in, crossed the interstate and looked there, too. "Where are you?" I hollered, but there was nothing there, no sound, no movement, no air.

A slash of lightning brought me to my senses. My knees

were shaking as I crossed the interstate. I began to laugh. A truck approached, saw my rig ahead, and came to a stop.

"Everything all right, driver?" he asked, as he walked toward me. He wasn't shocked to see a woman; hell, he'd heard about me, everyone had. Bobby had been proud of me.

"Just needed to wake up," I told him.

He glanced at the westward sky, the way we both had come, and regarded the storm. "Don't stay out here too long, Danny. This fucker's gonna hit with a mighty vengeance."

We walked side by side and he gave me a friendly slap on the shoulder. "You sure you're all right?"

I nodded. As an afterthought I said, "It must be the heat's getting the best of me." I forced a smile. "Being on the road again feels different. It's hard to shake these images that come to me."

He thought I was talking about Bobby. He said, "People say the past is here to haunt you for a reason, keeps you on track. The ghosts'll leave you alone. Just wait and see."

second law of thermodynamics
all systems tend toward disorder

People will tell you that you can't actually see heat, only the effect it has on things encompassed by it. Tarvia bubbles, earth dries, plants wilt, animals pant. But if anyone had been watching the snippet of time Dennis was killed, they would have seen the heat. For the few seconds I noticed it, I thought it was beautiful. Like small ocean waves. The swell, the crest, the conservative break. For a split second, I had the strange feeling that I'd spent the last twenty-eight years in a two-dimensional world, but now that heat had made me aware of its existence, everything visible, everything alive, had been suddenly inflated, as if someone had taken an air pump, stuck it against the needle of the world and given life to everything around me with one hard push.

I couldn't help but feel eerily intimate with it for a few seconds before it threw me back into the game. Like an overbearing parent losing control, it bore down on me again, and I could barely move through it. It would rather suffocate me than leave me unscathed.

The journalists couldn't move through the heat either, that's why it took them so long to get the story straight. They offered incorrect details about the trucks, how the accident took place, and what we did after Dennis was pronounced dead, like anyone really cared. What about the middle, when Heat had us by our throats, when we couldn't move fast enough? When the fumes from the tar were so thick in our eyes, we could scarcely see what we were doing? Once the journalists finally pulled free from the heat, who did they go to? The college kids. They asked the college kids for the story.

This was an opportunity for fame. They had no answers,

so they made up the facts. Threw in some soap-opera conflict. Talked about the trucks as if they were just contraptions, slabs of metal, grease and engines, instead of viable machines made like any other living thing, with skin, blood, and brains, that breathe and choke and tire out after a long day's work. I got tired of listening to them swear when the machines jerked and jolted, hummed, and rattled. *So do you*, I'd want to scream. I've seen you in the back seat of cars, your body twitching as you get bulldozed by your boyfriends. I've heard you gurgling in the break room as your girlfriends siphon the gas out of you. You are no different, I'd think.

That summer, I gave the college kids the same speech I had given the past couple years. "At times these machines can be as powerful as any one of Mother Nature's natural disasters," I'd said. "Treat them with the respect they deserve and they'll work for you till the bitter end. Fear them enough and they won't hurt you. Don't mess with the machines," I told them. "They can hurt you. I don't want that."

After I said it, I looked squarely at Dennis, who was standing with the full-timers, directly behind the semicircle of college kids. Dennis gave me a crude wag of the tongue. I'd rip it out of his mouth before I'd ever let it touch a spot of my skin, and he knew it.

"If you see something wrong with a machine," I continued, my gaze sliding back to the group, "you come to me, Buzz, Pip, Neil, Russ, Pete, Vic, or Ed." No mention of Dennis. He crossed his arms over his chest, and tapped his foot. He wasn't bright, but he was smart enough to know he'd been insulted.

The others were my friends. Some people considered the men I worked with to be as manufactured as the machines they drove. "Blue collar worker" was synonymous with "man without a brain." The ones who took shop instead of geometry; a male version of me, Danny, Dan. County workers were either big burly guys with mustaches or scrawny ones without teeth. And in our case, it was true, five to three. They were all good with their hands, though not a one ambitious. They all drove pickups that were beat to hell, looked at *Playboy*, smoked, and drank cheap beer that tasted like dog piss. But they were good people with more to them than greasy pants and stubbly faces, though they didn't have an urgent need to express this in public. Very few people, particularly our college workers, took the time to notice. In their eyes we were merely dumb, dirty county workers.

I showed the kids news clippings of road accidents, crushed machines and dead bodies; they grimaced, they half listened, it could never happen to them. I thought the same thing when I started driving, but Bobby's simple stories and disapproving looks taught me otherwise. Nobody's out of death's reach, he'd say.

I gave the kids a simple, linear $1 + 1$ equation: one bad judgment can cause—*will* cause—a negative chain of events. It's called cause and effect. You don't need to be a scientist to understand. After Dennis died, and my senses were running on overdrive, I began to dissect the incident until I came up with a new equation.

I broke Dennis's moment down to two equations, one that moved forward:

$1 + 1 + 1 + 1$, etc. $= 9$;

and translated into words:

Dennis didn't listen and he knew better; he climbed onto a machine I told him not to touch; he got crushed; we all got trapped in the heat; the reporters went to the college kids for the story; they told a story that wasn't true, throwing in details about blood and guts for good measure, and even a little heroics that wasn't there; their untruths made something mad, some cosmic force, some deity, some unknown evil step-sister of Mother Nature; their lies jinxed me.

And one that moved backward:

$9 - 1 = 8 - 1 = 7 - 1$ and so on $= 0$; or:

I became jinxed; the college kids made up stories; Dennis was killed; Dennis got onto a machine he was supposed to stay clear of; I got up late the morning of August 10 and didn't have time to read the newspaper; if I had, I would have read my horoscope as I did every morning, and maybe, just maybe, I would have heeded its advice and not gone to work; Dennis took one of the college girls to the salt shed and took advantage of her; Dennis buddied up with the kids until they ganged up on me and some of the other full-timers; the first morning the kids came to work for us, while I was giving my safety speech, I checked my watch to see if I had gone over, but the battery was dead, the watch stopped at 9:05, the exact time Dennis would die in the future; the roads were damaged because of the plows; this was the second worst winter in the second half of the century since 1966.

All this madness because of a bad winter; all this turmoil continued because of a small pack of lies. If only winter had been a tad bit milder; if only the journalists had come to me. Now this moment is locked inside my brain, my own personal movie theater, with surround sound, slow motion, freeze frame; an unceasing event that I think about as often as I smoke cigarettes.

collision-coalescence efficiency
the growth of cloud droplets that merge upon impact

By the time I got home that night I felt like I'd aged twenty years. My Chevy truck must have picked up the vibes because her body shuddered against the chassis when I pulled into the driveway. My muscles ache, she was saying. We're both tired, I thought, patting the dash. When I turned her off, she gave a final sigh and shake, then settled in for the night. She'd wake up in the morning. I wasn't so sure I would.

I had a small efficiency above a garage owned by Agnes Boyd, who was eighty-two. Agnes was always squinting at me, suspicious that I was throwing wild orgies after she went to bed. Her one rule was that I wasn't allowed to have boys in my room. Boys. Since I worked with all boys, it stood to reason I was actively sleeping with most of them. She was under the impression I was getting laid every night after her teeth came out. She sent her Maine Coon, Horace, to spy on me. He sat at the top of the steps, just outside my door, mewing like he was getting laid. I think she mistook his rapture for sex I wasn't having. I should have been able to sleep with anyone I wanted, whenever I wanted, though. After all, I was paying three hundred dollars a month for a garage apartment that smelled like gasoline. Three hundred dollars plus utilities to listen to her 1981 Cadillac babble every Sunday at 5:00 a.m., my only morning to sleep in. My first Sunday there, I was nearly asphyxiated by the carbon monoxide. After a narrow escape, I explained to her that she had to let the car warm up outside the garage or else she'd have my dead body to deal with.

Agnes wasn't a bad old crow, though. We had an agreement. She wouldn't raise my rent if I did some work around the house for her so I mowed the lawn, shoveled the driveway, fixed anything that was falling apart, kept her car tuned, dug up her garden every spring. After I saw her drive, I took up that chore too. Every Thursday afternoon I drove her to the grocery store. But when she tried to sway me into church one Sunday, I told her it was time to raise the rent.

Horace was sitting on the bottom step of the garage when I pulled in. He ran like hell to the house when the Chevy and I stopped twitching. As soon as my foot hit the stone pavement, I saw the curtain on the kitchen window fall into place. By the time I closed the truck door, Agnes was watching through a pane of glass in the kitchen door, frantically waving to get my attention. I was too worn out to deal with her, so I waved and headed for the stairs.

"Danny," she called through the glass and tapped with her fingernail. Her voice was muffled. It would sound the same when she haunted me from underground. "Come in here. I warmed some soup for you."

I stopped and took a deep breath. "I think I'm going to grab a shower and go to bed, Agnes. I've had a rough day."

Now she opened the door. "I know. I saw it on the news this afternoon. They didn't give names. I was worried. I thought it was you. I even called the county offices, just to make sure."

"That it was me?" I tried to joke, but Agnes's mouth was set in a pout, like a Bingo troll that had been discarded because it lost its luck.

"I was worried, Danny. You're all I've got left."

Why did she have to confess that? I liked us both better when we could tolerate each other only long enough to grocery shop. Her declaration was as heavy as the roller that pinned Dennis down, so I dropped to my knees and let the gravel grind into my hands, the stone embedding into my palms the way it did into Dennis's face. My mouth was open, my tongue dangling. Agnes rushed out and gripped my arm. She pulled a brown lunch bag out of her housecoat, her bag of tricks, and shoved it against my face.

"You're hyperventilating. Breathe into this," she instructed.

I looked over the bag at her face. There was makeup in her wrinkles that, by the looks of things, had been there for so long, it had packed into clay.

"How many times have I told you to quit that job. Go to the community college, learn to type."

Agnes tugged on my arm so many times, I buckled under her persistence and let her think she helped me to my feet. I followed her into her kitchen and waited for her to serve me homemade soup. Agnes had many flaws, most of which had to do with her religious affiliation, but despite them, she could still cook. Even in the heat, her hot soup tasted good, as though two negatives were making a positive. Every swallow felt like an adhesive trying to put me together again. After I ate, Agnes poured a couple cups of coffee percolated on the burner. It was official, I was tar on the inside and out.

"You probably want something stronger, but not here. You'll need to wait till you go back up there." She was indicating my apartment.

I pulled out a cigarette and raised my eyebrows.

"Go on, go on. You deserve it today."

She acted like her virginal walls had never seen a cigarette. She didn't know that from one of my little portholes, I could see directly into every room on the north side of her house. I'd seen her light up over the last few years, after her teeth were snug in their cup of water. With each drag her face looked as though it would collapse on itself, like a decayed orange. It was enough to make you want to quit smoking all together.

I held one out to her, but she gave me an insulted look.

"Suit yourself," I said, and smiled.

"You want to tell me what happened to your friend?"

"No. I can't, Agnes. And he wasn't my friend."

"I hope you haven't said that to anyone else today."

She had a point, but I wasn't going to admit it. "I'll tell you that I feel like everything's changed."

"How so? You finally going to register for a class at the community college?"

"I don't mean that kind of change. More like I'm loosening. Like, Jesus, I don't know, like the heat today melted my bone marrow and it's sloshing around inside me. Like my skin and bones are chattering."

"Did you stop off today with them other ones?" she asked.

I rubbed my face. My hands, I noticed, were dirty, spotted on the back with blood, and still smelled like tar. "No, but I'm beginning to wish I had."

"That feeling you're talking about, it happens to pregnant women. The pelvis loosens. Helps open the passageway. You," she said, taking a sip of coffee, "you don't have child bearing hips."

It was one of my flaws she liked to point out often.

"I don't know what you're going to do about it. Men like meat on bones, and women who stay at home."

If I were looking to be reeled into her argument, I'd have told her she was wrong, that every boyfriend I'd ever had was attracted to my skinniness, to my slightly androgynous features. That skinny, effeminate men gravitated to me. I'd have even admitted that I found that kind of man attractive or else I wouldn't have dated any of them. Instead, I stood; that was the only insult I was going to take tonight. I was too weary.

"How did it happen?" she tried, again.

I held my face in my hands, trying to erase the image of him.

"Really, Agnes. I just don't want to talk about it." No one deserved to hear the details of what he looked like, not even Agnes, but she hated not being the center of the gossip. What would she tell her friends on the phone after I left?

"It was gruesome." I decided to give her a little to keep her off my back.

"A lot of blood?"

"It wasn't so much about the blood."

"What was it then?"

It was more about the way everyone was looking at me, expecting me to do something. Glaring at me as though I should have stopped it before it had happened. Like I should have

known, like a mother knows before something bad happens
to her kid. Sixth sense was something I didn't possess, though
if Agnes had been on the job, she'd have seen it before it happened. She had that ability, the ability of knowing beforehand.

I leaned down on both hands against the table. A bead of
sweat rolled off the tip of my nose and landed on the table-
cloth. Agnes got at it with a dish towel as if it would stain.

"Get some rest. If you can't sleep, come down, I'll leave the
door unlocked."

"How many times do I have to tell you not to do that?"

"Well, if you need some company, I'll be up."

"Thanks, Agnes, but I have to work tomorrow."

"You're going back? How could you?"

"It's my job. I have to."

Even as I was ascending my steps, I felt like I was going in the
opposite direction, free falling. I felt like I had been dropped
out of a cloud and as I gained speed, I was smashing into droplets of water around me. My eyes were blurry, and as I walked
through my little home, I banged into pieces of furniture as
if they were bumpers in a pinball machine. How many points
had I accumulated? The light on my answering machine was
sending Morse code. I yanked it out of the wall and threw it in
the garbage. Inexplicably it still blinked, so I dropped it on the
floor and smashed it under my boot. I plopped down in the
kitchen chair, and looked at the newspaper, open to the comic
section where I had left it that morning. I lifted it and read my
horoscope, just to see.

*Sagittarius (Nov. 22-Dec. 21) Someone you conflict with is likely to
throw you a curve. You may not be able to contain the way you feel. It's time
to get rid of some of the dead weight in your life. Think about a lifestyle
change.*

Did taking typing classes constitute a lifestyle change? Agnes dished out more advice than my mother had, when she
was alive. Unfortunately, most of Agnes's advice was dated. If
it were up to her, every woman in the country would still be

tethered by an apron from waist to stove. She was as mortified by my occupation as my mother had been. If they had known each other, I believe they would have conspired against me.

Glancing back at my horoscope I wondered, if this one day had been predicted, could I trace my experiences up to this point, chart them the way a meteorologist charts weather behavior to find a pattern, and make my own predictions? I'd paid little attention to what the astrologers said the stars had in store for me, but now I wondered if someone or something was leaving clues, and I felt a sudden need to find the hidden message. Had I been born into an unlucky life, or was I truly in control of the helm?

I found a pad of paper and a pen and jotted down moments that had stuck with me over the years. Chronology was irrelevant, I'd do that later.

"Okay, my first lesson in Gendernomics," I said aloud.

...I am sitting on the floor at the doctor's office, pushing a truck back and forth, pretending I'm a driver like my dad. The mother of a boy who is playing with a doll on the floor next to me snatches the truck from my hands.

"Girls play with dolls and boys play with trucks," she scolds, before ripping the doll from her son's arms. I look up at my mother standing at the counter, hoping she's going to intervene, but she's caught up talking with the receptionist.

The boy and I stare at each other. I have no idea what to do with the doll, and by the way he holds the truck in the palm of his hand, he's just as baffled by it. We both steal a glance at his mother, the toy gender police, then back at each other. We shuffle across the carpet closer and closer. He places the truck down and I put the doll on top of it. Immediately my hand slips down to grasp the cold metal, and his holds the doll on for the ride.

...I am a seventeen-year-old grocery store cashier, and my nineteen-year-old boyfriend is the bagger. He's what my father would consider a pansy. He has let me dominate him from day one. It's been a steady courtship, with lots of kissing and lots of

outside the clothes petting. When that grows boring, we take it
to his bedroom. I'm still a virgin, but I've seen the movies, the
magazines; my hormones are at a boiling point, it's time to take
the plunge.

He takes his shirt off. His chest is smooth, hairless and pale,
the small nickel-sized nipples like two brown birthmarks. From
now until I die, I will crave my men like this: girlie, feminine,
and smooth. He wants to undress me, but I have seniority over
this body so I do it myself. He flops down on the bed and
watches.

He says, "Will you be on top?" I have no issue with that
yet; it still gives me control. I straddle his stomach and pretend to be a car on a hydraulic lift. I wonder what he'll do, oil
change and lube, tune up, alignment, I'm in need of all. He's all
thumbs, fumbling with the parts. His tongue works properly
in his mouth, he's able to carry on a civilized conversation, but
now it's ineffective. He doesn't know the difference between
the throttle and the brake; he has no career opportunity in mechanics.

He holds himself in his hand and says assertively, "Get on."
I start to, but then I remember. I'm not going to inflict pain and
impale myself on dear Vlad below me.

"You're going to have to do this," I say. "I'm a virgin."

He seems a bit put off, not that I'm a virgin, but that he has
to work a little. He isn't the most energetic or efficient bagger,
either.

I live through the discomfort with my eyes squeezed together as he goes on and on and on. He seems incapable of ejac-
ulating, seems to be getting harder rather than softer. Doesn't
this go against some law of physics? Or gravitational force?
Or angle of friction? Isn't there a formula or a word problem
scientists use to figure out how long it takes?

Two trains leave two different stations at the same time.
They are heading on the same track toward each other. One
train is going fifty miles per hour, the other fifty-five. The train
traveling at fifty-five has one male and one female passenger.

They are screwing at approximately twice the speed as the first train is traveling. If the man has a six-inch cock with an inch and a half width and is moving at record pace inside a hole just about the size of a large marble, shouldn't it, at some point, finally explode?

Listen, Vlad, you've caused enough friction to start a forest fire, let's get on with it.

He pulls out, his penis red, screaming for release, but instead of finishing himself off, he fishes under his bed.

"Put this on," he says and buckles me into a contraption. I have a good seven inches myself, now. He lubes it up and says, "Be gentle," before he gets on all fours. What to do? I try to insert it into a hole not meant for such large objects. We start again and I'm going at him and I have to say I'm enjoying it. It's the control, the choice to pull and push him against me, or drive myself into him. Vlad the Impaled.

"Thanks for the experience," I tell him once his penis has finally exhaled, and I've pulled out of his backside.

"Want me to do it to you?" he asks with such kindness I almost say yes. But I can't bear the sight of his poor penis holding its breath again.

"Maybe next time," I tell him.

I'd listed only two memories, and was tired already. Poor Vlad. Poor me.

I went into the bathroom to look in the only mirror in my apartment.

"How did you get here?" I asked my reflection. "You went on a run and so did some fucker coming from Washington state. He was a greedy bastard and wanted the money more than the sleep he needed. In his speed-induced state, he crossed the median and completely crushed your parents. You demanded to see the bodies, they told you it would be better if you didn't, they requested dental records. You sold their house, cashed in the small life insurance policies, settled the case outside of court, all that money was useless to you, so you put it in the bank, found the smallest apartment on earth, bought used furniture from the Salvation Army and settled for a job with the county. That's how you got here. Since you seem to have all the answers, tell me this: where do I go from here?"

"Danny?"

I turned and saw Buzz standing in the kitchen watching me talk to myself in the bathroom mirror. He held my keys up before I could ask. "You left 'em in the door. You okay? I've been calling, but the machine didn't pick up."

"I accidentally dropped it."

Buzz looked at the mutilated machine on the floor, its guts hanging out. "That musta been one hell of a fall."

He held out a bottle of Southern Comfort. "Deena thought you could use a sleep enhancer."

"What time is it? Eleven, twelve?"

Buzz looked at his watch. "Just about nine."

"Jesus, that early. Did Agnes see you coming up? Never mind, I don't care, let's drink."

Buzz poured a couple shots and we sat down at the table.

"Call in tomorrow," Buzz said.

"Can't."

"The kids aren't coming back, you know that, right?"

"Fucking cowards."

"Smart fucking cowards."

I nodded. "Let's go out back. I need some air."

"Want me to hide this?" he asked, holding up the bottle.

I emptied its contents into two large plastic cups and we slipped outside as quietly as we could. Agnes was watching, I could feel her. I stepped on Horace, kind of by accident, but mostly on purpose, just to hear him yelp.

Buzz pulled my seat out and sat heavily in his. He took a good long look at me in the dark. The end of our cigarettes looked like lightning bugs, the puff and glow, puff and glow, intrusive and calming all at once. Buzz lit himself a fresh one from the one still in his mouth.

He said, "I can't stop thinking about it, Danny."

I nodded, even though it was dark. He knew that's what I'd

do. I suppose that's why, since Bobby's death, he was as close to a best friend as I would ever have.

"You too?" he asked, before coughing deep smoker rattles. Buzz was one of the burly guys. He towered over me somewhere around six foot, four inches. His arteries were roughly the size of fire hoses, all the more cigarettes he could smoke before they were clogged, lucky dog.

"What are you thinking about most of all?"

He shrugged then sucked so hard on the cigarette I thought the crackle would ignite his fingers. "Oh, you know."

"How the hell could I?" I asked.

He said, "Teeth. I've been thinking about his teeth."

I nodded because I seemed to remember pulling a few out of Dennis's mouth when he was pinned by the machine. "They were too small for a grown man's mouth, don't you think? Small and hard."

"Did you think so too?" he asked, turning to me.

This should have been something to laugh at, but we didn't.

"Hell," he said, thinking about it. "Oh hell."

"Anything else?" I pushed, because the more I drank and got lost in the thickness of the booze, the quicker the truth would sink in.

"Just the teeth, really. And maybe—" But he stopped.

"What else?" I asked and sat up.

He shook his head and laughed a little. "It was just one of those things that went through my head for a second."

"What things?"

But Buzz shook his head again. "It'll sound wrong," he said, his voice so deep he could've been growling.

"Say it anyway."

"When I first jumped out of my truck…well, I don't know, Danny. After it happened, all I saw was you standing there looking down at him with a smirk on your face. Then I saw the teeth."

A smirk? Why would I have been smirking? I didn't have time to smirk. As soon as the machine went into the ditch, I ran like hell to see if he was all right. I didn't have time to smirk, to swear, or to shit my pants. It happened too fast.

Buzz lit me a cigarette and said, "It was too crazy to know what really happened."

I felt as if the wind had been knocked out of me. It was no secret that Dennis and I had hated each other. Sworn enemies. But even in this state, the state of hatred, the state where every time Dennis was within ten feet of me, my body tensed like a cat's, I wouldn't have smirked.

"I don't think it was a smirk. Maybe shock. You know, Buzz? Shock?"

"We've been doing this too long," he stated plainly, skirting the answer.

One winter when we had been sitting in our truck watching the snow fall, waiting for the predicted lake effect, we'd discussed our futures and Buzz told me it was time to retire when you knew where every crack, bump, and pothole was on every road in the county. He said it was something like your wife's body. As the years go on, it begins to wear, though you don't necessarily love it less; but you cover it and you cover it until, finally, there are so many war wounds you just give up, and either avoid them or accept them for what they are. Was that a realization that came with age, one that was acceptable and even embraced once it happened, or was it a bleak fact of life? Both choices seemed undesirable to me. Dismal. Boring. There had to be something more than routine and constraints.

Buzz was living proof that there wasn't. He'd been at this job for twenty years and was still driving a ten-wheel dump truck. When the foreman position became available a few years ago, he didn't bid it himself, which he should have done. Instead, he suggested me to his father-in-law, who was one of the men upstairs. They were apprehensive because I was a woman. They didn't say that, though. They were too smart to say something like that. They said it was because of my tenure. I had started in August of '91, so I'd only been on the job for nine months. There were others who were less qualified, but more tenured.

Buzz pointed out that four of the six men were close to retire-
ment and the other two weren't all that quick on their feet. One,
of course, was Dennis.

It was decided I would go through a training period where
I'd be the foreman of the summer oiling crew. In the history of
the county, no man had ever gone through this kind of testing.
While I knew it was unfair, I had never considered myself an
active feminist and causing a stink would not help me get the
job. Plus, I just didn't care. I was healing from all the death in
my life, and I was too tired to fight. I agreed to the conditions
and took on the responsibility. And now, three years later, I was
about to be buried with it.

"Danny? Danny?"

"Hmm?"

"I said, you've been staring into space for ten minutes.
Where are you?"

I was hurling through space as a new member of the Hy-
drologic Cycle cult. At some point today I had evaporated and
drifted into the sky, jumped from cloud formation to rain cloud,
and now I was incognito, disguised as precipitation heading for
the ground. The ground was growing closer and closer. It was
only a matter of time before we collided.

cusp
a pointed end where two curves meet

Whenever I need to feel more environmentally aware, I carry a load to Texas. In Texas I never, no matter what, throw cigarette butts out the window. I figure the one time I do, a line of fire will follow behind my truck, and lead the police right to me. The heat in Texas is different than the heat in New York. Texas is dry, crispy, crumbly. A cigarette on the thruway is as lethal as a match in hay. New York heat is saturating, boiling, drowning. One dissolves, one engulfs, and yet in both you end up in the same mental state.

When I left the county, Buzz gave me the homemade ceramic ashtray that was in our truck, as a going away gift. "It'll keep you from throwing your cigarettes out the window," he said. Even though he was as adamant about not littering as I was, I knew he was really just trying to be tough about my leaving. Then he scratched his mustache and his tone softened. "Maybe you'll think about me once in a while," he said, rubbing at his eyes so I wouldn't see the tears. Deena wasn't as secretive about it. She wiped them off her cheeks as they fell, hugging me over and over. She packed me a basket of food. They were sending me off like Dorothy.

Barley, an English Bulldog, kept trying to break free from the leash Buzz's son, Jeff, was holding. The kids bought him for me three Christmases ago, but he played a little too rough with Horace, so Agnes told me I had to get rid of him after a whole year as a couple. It's only fair, she had said, Horace was here first. And so, the kids parented him for me. Now that I was leaving, I knew I'd never regain custody. The sad reality was that I really loved him. Barley knew I was leaving. He wanted to come with me, and I wanted to take him, more than anything.

But I wasn't about to take the pet away from my best friend's children.

It's all right, boy, I said, jiggling the thick flesh around his jowls. He nuzzled his nose into my neck and I held him tight. I didn't want to let him go. He didn't want me to, either.

After our hug, Barley shook his skin out and the dog tags chimed against the metal clasp of his collar. It was a comforting sound, one that had always soothed me when we had lived together. He panted and ambled slowly when Jeff pulled the leash, giving me one more backward glance. Agnes was watching from the kitchen door window. She was sulking and she wouldn't come out. Horace was also conspicuously missing, but then I don't know if that was because he was pouting too, or if it was because Barley was present; probably the latter.

I waved to her and she let the curtain fall as though she hadn't seen me.

Deena said, "Go talk to her."

"Nah," I said. "She's mad at me. She gets mean when she's mad."

"Harry'll take care of things," Buzz reassured me, but it wasn't me who needed convincing.

Harry was Buzz's brother. He and his wife were splitting up so it worked out for all of us. We didn't tell Agnes about the divorce because she would never let a sinner live in her garage.

Deena pushed me toward the house and I ambled as slowly as Barley, giving Agnes time to load insults into her barrel. At first, she wouldn't open the door. She was holding her ninety-pound self against it, trying to keep me from coming in. I gave a very small nudge, so I wouldn't hurt her already fragile hips, and she moved. She turned away so I wouldn't see she'd been crying.

I said, "It's okay to be sad, Agnes."

She said, "I'm sad all right. I'm sad because I won't be seeing you in heaven."

"You never know," I told her. "I might die before you."

"It doesn't matter when you die," she said, exasperated by

my stupidity. "You could die tomorrow and I still won't see you in heaven."

Thinking this was a joke, I said, "Okay, why won't you see me in heaven," and prepared to laugh.

"Because you haven't saved yourself. You just drive further and further into badness."

"Do you really want me to leave like this?"

"That's your problem. You don't think you live like a sinner."

"I haven't done anything wrong, Agnes."

"Your lifestyle is wrong; your job is wrong."

"All truckers are sinners?"

She wouldn't answer.

"What did I do for you last night?" I asked her.

"I don't know what you're talking about," she said quietly.

"At three this morning."

"You went to the store for graham crackers."

"Why?"

"Because my stomach hurt."

"And?"

"And graham crackers with milk settle my stomach. So what?"

"And where did the store get the crackers?"

"From the manufacturer. I still don't see your point?"

"From the manufacturer? You mean to tell me, that little box of graham crackers walked itself from…" I searched the cupboard for the box and read the packaging label. "…from New Jersey."

She wouldn't say no. So I said, "A sinner like me drove it to the store so a sinner like me could go out in the middle of the night so you'd have crackers to dunk in your milk so your tummy wouldn't hurt."

"It's dangerous out there, Danny. You're going to get yourself hurt, then what'll I do?"

"Harry's a good guy, Agnes. I promise he'll take care of you. I made out a list of everything he needs to do and the days you want them done. He's very handy. And besides, he's a man, he'll probably do it better than me."

"What am I going to do when my crackers run out?" she asked, ignoring my crack.

"I'll have delivered a new load by then."

Agnes said, "Pull the door behind you."

I'm carrying a load of lawn chairs to Dallas, Texas, listening to a tape of the Beatles' greatest hits. It's basically a straight shot, just shy of a thousand miles, so I can concentrate on the lyrics and not fret over missed exits. I rewind "I Want to Hold Your Hand" over and over. It's as far as I got with Jesse before I left South Carolina, and I feel nearly impregnated by the contact. Lucky, happy, blessed. But blessings have never relieved me of my superstitions. Through Georgia, Alabama, Mississippi, Louisiana, and Texas, I remember all my superstitious routines. I hold my breath past cemeteries, through tunnels, over bridges. I lift my feet over railroad tracks. I'm as good as gold even through Louisiana.

I can't keep from feeling that Jesse is my good luck charm. Hell, if I could I'd hang him like a rabbit's foot from the belt loop of my jeans. But with Jesse it's going to be slow. There were times during our conversations when I felt like I was getting somewhere, like I'd managed to pull back a layer and get a little deeper inside Jesse's complex being, but then another secret would grow visible, like skin healing itself—skin like plastic wrap, clear but lasting, see-through but virtually impenetrable—and I'd have to start all over again. It'll be like eating an artichoke, one leaf at a time. And really, when I think about it, I'm wealthy with time. I settle my shoulders into the seat, my truck is as comfortable on I20 as a train on a track, so I can revisit the last couple days with Jesse without interruption.

...I'm awake at five a.m. and walk stealthily down the hall. I don't so much as peek at the other doors for fear of being caught. I'm surprised to see the Employees Only door open to the bar. Jesse is sitting alone at a round table, smoke swirling around his head, the Beatles playing softly from the juke box.

I couldn't find a sexier scene if I searched for one, I think to myself.

He's punching numbers into a calculator.

I clear my throat and he looks up from the ledger.

"You certainly are an early bird," he says, with that fine southern Alabama drawl.

He indicates the chair next to him and I practically leap into it.

"You too," I say.

Jesse shrugs. "I sleep four hours a night. I don't like being in the state of sleep."

"Leaves you vulnerable," I add because I know better than anyone, and Jesse nods.

"And how *did* you sleep? Fine, I hope."

I nod.

"Would you like a cup of coffee?"

"Is it instant or the real thing?" I ask.

"Northerners," he says, shaking his head and then smiling.

I push my chair back to help myself, but like a well-trained housewife, he pats my arm and goes behind the bar. He pours fresh cups for both of us and comes back carefully, watching so he doesn't spill.

"My father taught me that if you don't look at the liquid, it won't go over."

"Is that right?" Jesse says, and puts the cups down. "I'll have to try that next time. You need cream or sugar?" *Shuga* it sounds like, and I dissolve into the word as if I've been tossed into the coffee myself.

I shake my head and he sits down again.

"What else did your daddy teach you?" he teases.

"How to work with my hands," I say. "How to drive a truck." How to be lonely.

Jesse nods appreciatively.

"What did your father teach you?" I ask.

Jesse holds a pack of cigarettes out to me with one already sticking up. I lean forward and he lights it, and then his.

"How to smoke."

"Sounds like he's a man with taste."

"Not really," Jesse adds, with a hint of disgust, saying nothing more.

We reach a dead end at about the same time "Something" comes on. A good omen, I think.

I say, "I thought southerners like country music."

Jesse nods and drags deep. The smoke shoots out in a long steady stream, like fire from a dragon.

"I'm not like most southerners," he says with a serious tone. "Unless, of course, I'm feeling sorry for myself, then I put on some Patsy Cline." He smiles at me, and I swear he's flirting, but then he looks back at the calculator.

"I guess I'll head to the garage, see how my rig's doing," I announce flatly.

Rather than looking at the watch face on his wrist, Jesse pulls his pocket watch out and says, "It's 5:17 in the morning. This might be a stretch, but I do not think the garage is open yet."

"Well," I say, because now I can't leave. I look down at the ledger. "You doing the books for Gary?"

"For Gary?" He glances up at me quizzically and then smiles again. "That's right, I'm just calculatin' last night's numbers."

"Does the bar turn a good profit?"

"This may surprise you, but between the rooms and the bar, it does. We're usually full five, six nights a week."

"Gary mentioned something about a show last night."

Jesse laughs. "Yes, well, it's not really a show. There's a ten-thirty singing of 'Yellow Submarine.' We like to pay homage to our namesake. Something small, something simple, that's all."

The juke box drops "Ticket to Ride" and we stare at each other; something small, something simple, but that's not all. My body parts are as potent as a jet engine. The heat inside me is about to project me out of the chair.

"Let's go for a ride," Jesse says, as though he reads my mind.

My first thought is to grab him by the hand and run him to the bedroom, but then I realize he means something different.

I'm flexible. I've had sex just about everywhere imaginable…a janitor's closet, the bed of my plow. I had a lover who could only get it on to the sound of his parakeets chirping. We all have our fetishes. If Jesse's is the outdoors, then I'll declare that outdoor sex is just as refreshing.

He hands me a black leather motorcycle jacket with buckles and zippers, one that has been cared for and molded to his body for so long that it wraps around my bones like a sheath. We slip out the side door and walk a gravel path to a garage behind the bar. He lifts the door and there they are, two Harley's, like fraternal twins. The '69 Panhead I saw last night and a '58 Duo-Glide. If I were alone, I'd drop to my knees and weep.

"Oh my," I say, and run my hand up and over the sissy bar as I did last night.

"You like it?" Jesse says as if he's relieved.

"She's the single most beautiful machine I've ever seen." But then I face the Duo-Glide and I have to retract my statement. "They both are."

"I have a third, a '93 Softail. But she's getting a tune up." Jesse wheels the Panhead out, straddles it, and bounces down on the kick start. "Do you want a helmet?" he calls over the engine.

This ride needs to be experienced in a natural state.

"I didn't come out of my mother with a helmet on," I say, and grip Jesse around the waist as I climb on.

"Amen to that," he says, and hits the throttle.

We ride and ride, about two hours, until we get to the ocean. My hair, which is light brown and straight, just past my ears, is windblown off my forehead. Jesse's has stayed the same. We sing Beatles songs the whole way, screaming them into the wind, not exactly hearing each other, or even knowing, really, if we're singing the same songs at the same time, but the vibrations are enough. Details don't matter.

At some point, I don't remember when, Jesse puts on sunglasses and indicates for me to check the pocket of the jacket I'm wearing. And then we sing some more. I'm surprised I remember all the lyrics, but it's like that with the Beatles. We're somewhere between Myrtle Beach and Charleston, the masculine and feminine of South Carolina's coastal towns. I don't know exactly where, and I don't ask. Usually when I don't have control of the helm, I feel lost, but today is different. I've put myself in Jesse's hands, and I feel safe.

We stop and walk to the shore and Jesse takes a deep breath, as if he's letting the ocean know he's there.

"'While I breathe, I hope,'" he declares, as though he's a paid advertisement for South Carolina. Then he gives me a look like I'm insulting our hostess so I take a deep breath too. The salty air has to bypass obstacles of nicotine but it goes in, and once it's finally there, I exhale loudly.

We both bend at the same time to pick up shells and rocks. We look at each other and laugh. We study our finds, then switch at the same time and pocket each other's discoveries.

"You have a girlfriend?" I ask. It slips through what I thought are closed lips.

Jesse doesn't look at me. Instead, he looks out at the waves. "Nope."

"A boyfriend?" It squeaks out because the wrong answer will hurl me into the sea.

"Nope."

He doesn't ask so I say, "Me either." Jesse nods, or maybe he just looks back at the sand.

We follow the shoreline to a small break-wall. We have to hop from rock to rock to get to the end. Jesse is in his biker boots and I'm wearing Timberlands. We are, for sure, an odd-looking couple. A pair of masculine women, a pair of feminine men. He takes his jacket off and puts it down for us to sit on. Our arms touch. The very essence of him stings me.

"I had this thought," I say.

He doesn't ask what it is, just looks out at the waves. There are times when I've wished for the passive trait my mother and Agnes and so many other women inherited, but as it was passing by, it looked down, shook its head, and kept moving.

One night after a boy broke up with me, I was in the garage replacing an alternator, and my father came in to help. We worked in silence for a while before he asked where my boyfriend was. I told him what had happened, that the boy said I was too bossy, too impatient.

My father handed me a wrench and said, "It's funny the way it goes. Men spend the first fifth of their lives controlled by their mothers, the third fifth controlled by their wives, the fourth fifth controlled by their daughters, and the last by their granddaughters."

"What about the second fifth?" I asked, reaching in to unplug the electrical connector.

"That's where girlfriends come in. It's the only time in a guy's life when the girl is just as confused and unsure, if not more so, than the boy. I think it's the only time in life when men actually have some control over their own lives. Don't forget to disconnect the battery."

"I know," I reminded him. "Is that why so many teenage girls get pregnant?"

He seemed surprised by the question but he thought about it. "Probably is."

"Do you think I should change?" I asked.

My father handed me the new alternator. "What would happen to a car without the charge of the alternator?"

"The battery would go dead. The car wouldn't run."

"Every car needs an alternator," he said.

I want to study Jesse but I learned last night that that kind of examination makes him as nervous as a shy schoolgirl. Instead, I stare at my hands. They look empty without a cigarette and I need one so badly. Jesse pulls a pack out of his shirt pocket and lights two.

"I swear it's like you can read my mind," I say, unsettled.

He takes a long drag and then leans back on his right elbow. His left knee is bent, his right foot hangs off the rock and jiggles. He's still looking out at the ocean. Perhaps this is an indication that I should keep my mouth shut, but every battery needs a charge.

"I was thinking that maybe somewhere along the way whether it be here and now, or maybe later on once we get back—whatever's good for you, because either would be good for me—that maybe we could kiss just once."

He takes another drag then squashes the cigarette out on the rock. I put my hand out to take it, because I don't want him throwing it into the sea, and he smiles. Not at me, but at my action. He takes a plastic baggy out of his coat pocket and drops it in. He waits for me to finish mine, then I do the same. I note that the two cigarette butts have had more contact than we have. It would be pitiful to be jealous of a sea-soaked cigarette butt.

"When I retire, I'm going to live out here," he says.

"Retire? Retire from what, helping Gary pour beer once a week?" I tease.

Jesse sits up and studies me. He looks confused.

"Oh, that's right," he says, shaking his head. "I keep forgetting I'm the freeloader who lives off Gary."

He laughs and jumps off the break wall. He's left everything behind so I assume he's coming back. Jesse scours the ground, picking up rocks, inspecting them, then throwing them back again. He finds one and scrutinizes it. Satisfied, he goes all the way to the beginning of the break-wall then hops back toward me.

He settles himself down again, takes my hand and holds it palm up.

"You've come from out of nowhere, Danny Fletcher."

I don't recall my mother ever having taught me how to respond to a statement like that so I keep quiet.

"I love the ocean, Danny. It's where I belong and someday, I'm going to come back to it and live. I really am," he insists, as though I've challenged him. He's still holding my hand, but he's staring out at the horizon. "I got this for you," he says and puts a smooth rock in my palm. It's black and oval shaped, except there's a small, rounded tumor-like appendage to it. One side is impressed, as if someone has rubbed an indentation into it. "This rock probably had all kinds of ridges and gullies, and the sea eroded them away till it became smooth like this."

"It's lucky in a way. It's gotten to experience different shapes."

"Is that what you think?"

"Sure, why not."

"Would you say that someone who lost an arm or leg is lucky because he's gotten to experience different shapes?"

I shrug. I think about Barley and frown because I miss the way he snorts when I talk to him. I don't know why it hasn't occurred to me before now, but I finally decide to give my truck a name: Old Snort, after Barley.

"I had a dog that was neutered and he doesn't seem to suffer."

"Is that a fact?"

"Well, I guess I don't know for certain. But I don't love him less because of it."

"Maybe it isn't about you loving him. Maybe it's about him being able to love himself."

"All right, I'll buy that even though he's a dog, but then there's this. It's something I've been thinking about lately. Maybe he was born to be this way. Maybe it's his fate."

Jesse's eyes go back out to the horizon and he recites, "'Has any one supposed it lucky to be born? I hasten to inform him or her it is just as lucky to die, and I know it. I pass death with the dying and birth with the new-wash'd babe, and am not contain'd between my hat and boots...'"

"Did you make that up?" I ask, impressed.

Jesse smiles. "It's a poem by Walt Whitman. It's called 'Song of Myself.'"

"You went to college," I say, disheartened.

"No. I'm self-educated."

"Go on. Tell me more."

"'Every kind for itself and its own, for me mine male and female,/For me those that have been boys and that love women,/For me the man that is proud and feels how it stings to be slighted,/For me the sweet-heart and the old maid, for me mothers and the mothers of mothers,/For me lips that have smiled, eyes that have shed tears,/For me children and the be-getters of children.'"

Jesse takes the smooth ocean rock from my hand and kisses the impressed side. "This is the only kiss I can give you," he tells me, and he seems as sad to say it as I am to hear it.

"I'll take it," I say, and he presses it to my lips.

I taste the salt of the sea that is the salt of his lips; I tell my-self that I'll lick through his secrets and consume the offensive taste of his secrecy because beneath it I'm sure I know what his soul is made of.

I'm anxious to get back to South Carolina. I've lied in my log-book about the number of hours and miles I've gone, but we all do. Going from here to there in the shortest amount of time possible is simply a must. The less time it takes to deliver a load, the more runs we can make. The more runs we make, the more money we pocket. This is simple math. This is our livelihood, I announce to the skeptics in my brain, who argue my true motivation. There is a brief silence, giving the truth of the declaration time to settle and then disappear before this voice I've never heard before clears its throat and says modestly, *The shortest distance from Texas to Kansas City, Missouri, is not via South Carolina.* Mind your business, I say to myself.

My agenda changed when my rig broke. It took two days to fix, two days I got to spend with Jesse. Instead of going directly to Kansas City, Missouri, I go back to South Carolina where Jesse and I sit in the bar until four in the morning, talking about two things: this theory about reincarnation that Jesse finds interesting, and Mr. Walt Whitman. I tell him that I had a boyfriend who wrote Shakespeare's love poems to me.

"Sonnets," he corrects.

"Those too," I say. "That boy talked as fast as he screwed. It was hard to pay attention. I'm a good listener when I'm inter-ested." I hint and steal a glance at him. "He wanted me to know everything about him." Yet I wanted nothing but physical. It was easier that way.

But Jesse, he's different. A puzzle, a mystery, and the more distance he keeps between us, the more I want to know.

Jesse talks too, he talks in riddles, he answers with Whitman, "'...You are also asking me questions and I hear you, I answer that I cannot answer, you must find out for yourself.'"

We had exactly eighteen hours together, but now I've left for Missouri, Arkansas, Missouri, Oklahoma, back to Texas. The farther west I head, the more I think about him, and the more I crave the words of Walt Whitman that come out of the mouth of Jesse Reid. I dream of his hands, his long thin fingers, the way he wears a flannel shirt over a T-shirt, of the way his thick hair stays slicked back, the way he bats his eyelashes when he's nervous. About thirty miles before the Louisiana border, I hit a truck stop for some brew, and go through the postcard rack for Buzz's kids. I get one from every city and state I make a delivery in. But something different catches my eye. It's one of James Dean, where he's walking down a road, dressed in khaki pants, a white T-shirt, and a tan blazer. His hands are half in his pockets, bent backward at the joints. His eyes are looking down. A cigarette hangs out of one side of his mouth and his look is a serious one. It's his hair, though. Just like Jesse's. I buy it and tape it to my visor.

Every two days I call Harry to see how he's holding up, then I call Agnes to see what she's put the poor man through. I've been gone more than two months and she still won't let him drive her to the grocery store. I give him a list of items she usually buys, and he leaves them at the kitchen door. He tells me that he hides behind a tree and watches her open the door, look around to make sure the coast is clear, then snatch them up. I'll tell him to give her time. She's a tough old crow, but she'll give in. I ask Agnes how's she been getting to church. She's driven herself a few times, but the last time she put the car in a ditch and then hitched home instead of calling Harry. Fortunately, a cop picked her up.

I scold her. "Some lunatic could have picked you up and killed you."

"It's better than being killed by that hairy man."

"His name's Harry, Agnes. He isn't actually hairy."

"How do you know?" she questions. "He goes out back there without a shirt on. His pants hang down and I can see the crack of his rear end. Don't tell me he isn't hairy."

I huff into the phone.

She says, "When are you coming back? He isn't snowplowing the driveway the way I like. The back gate squeaks. The window in my bedroom is jammed."

"Don't be stubborn, Agnes. He's Buzz's brother. He's a good guy."

"I know all about that friend of yours. Who can trust a man with a name that ridiculous?"

"It's a nickname. If you feel more comfortable calling him Hubert, go ahead."

"Hubert? What kind of a name is that?"

"Precisely," I say.

"It doesn't matter anyway. He's got all them kids, and that disgusting dog."

"Barley is mine," I remind her. "Listen, I've put a package in the mail for you. Some stuff I've picked up here and there. Make sure you open the door for the postman."

"Bring it to me yourself."

"I can't. But I want to tell you something. I've met someone, Agnes."

"Who?"

"His name is Jesse."

"He's not good enough for you."

"He's too good for me," I say.

"Is he Catholic?"

"I don't think so," I tell her. "Maybe Baptist or Methodist. I'm not sure, though."

"At least you won't be lonely in hell," she says, and hangs up. I know she's happy for me.

❧

Jesse has taught me about the Wheel of Rebirth. He believes that life is only life because it comes from the opposite state, which, of course, is death. Life has to die before it can live again. I used chickens to argue my point.

"If a chicken lays an egg, and you eat the egg, a new chicken doesn't come out of it."

"Without the chicken you have no egg," Jesse said. "And without the egg you have no chicken. One egg always survives. It's all about rebirth."

He says that the Wheel of Life is divided into light and dark, and our souls pass from one to the other. We pass through once as human, then through again as a different form.

This interaction, like most of the others, was late, after the bar was closed. It was just us and the Beatles. Jesse poured a couple beers while I dug through my pocket for my ocean rock. I held it to my cheek. Then I said that butterflies were born one thing and then reincarnated into something else entirely. Jesse agreed but also argued that, although they were similar, there was a distinct difference between reincarnation and meta-morphosis. That rebirth means new forms and metamorphosis means transformation of the same form.

Jesse said, "This reminds me of a story. Hermes and Aph-rodite. They had a son who they named Hermaphroditus." There was no recognition in my stare. So he said, "When he was fifteen, he started poking around and came across a fountain called Salmacis. This pool of water was as clear as glass and in it was a water-nymph, also named Salmacis, and when she saw Hermaphroditus, she was instantly determined to get to know him."

"She was horny."

He chuckled and said, "That's right, she was aroused by him. But besides that, he was said to be remarkably handsome, his body as perfect as an ivory statue. Unfortunately, he didn't want anything to do with her and he threatened to leave. Afraid that she'd be left without him, Salmacis told Hermaphroditus that she'd leave him alone so he could swim. But instead, she hid behind some bushes and watched him strip and dive into the water. She couldn't contain herself, so she stripped down naked and dove in after him. Once she caught hold of him, she wouldn't let go."

"Maybe he liked other boys," I suggested.

Jesse blushed and continued. "She prayed to the gods that they never be separated. And the gods heard her prayers and the two bodies merged together as one. 'Two beings, and no longer man and woman, but neither, and yet both.'"

"Interesting story."

"Indeed, it is."

"How does it end?"

"Hermaphroditus said that the waters of Salmacis were contaminated so he prayed to his mother and father that anyone who swam in the water would emerge half man."

"Because being half woman is a punishment," I scoffed. "What does this have to do with what we're talking about?"

"Metamorphosis. Changing forms."

I smoked half a cigarette before I said, "There doesn't seem to be any light at the end of this darkness."

Jesse told me I was born a pessimist.

When I reach Louisiana, I realize I've allowed myself to believe in misconceived luck, which has given me a sense of false security. I've been back on the road for six days and it's gotten to the point where I'm afraid to close my eyes. The victims from the roadside come in and watch me when my eyes are closed. At least when I'm awake I can see them watching me. There's only one thing to do, and that's to stop sleeping, which I did a couple of days ago. In Tennessee the unimaginable happens, and I'm angry with myself because I should have expected it. Up ahead I see Bobby's rig jackknife, slide, and flip on its side. It skids across the pavement ahead of me. The black dog whirls to face me, to take me head on, and I hit my brake. My trailer becomes so heavy it feels like a herd of elephants is pushing me forward.

"Bobby!" I yell at the windshield, but he is nearly cut in two, inside the cab of his truck. I let my foot off the brake, and, gripping the wheel, aim for the dog. "I'll take you, fucker," I holler, and the grill of my truck whooshes through him, shattering his reflection. He's behind me now, barking and snarling, and I'm so afraid, I press down on the accelerator, not caring how fast I'm going on the mountain. But I can't get away. They're out in full force, and they're chasing me.

I've let my guard down by daydreaming about Jesse, and now I can't stop thinking this: you know better, you know better, you know better. It's what I chant to stay awake.

What do you know, really? I ask myself. Your thoughts are no longer your own, they scatter and scurry like centipedes, and stand by the crosses and wait to be noticed. When you don't acknowledge them, they run after you. You hit the gas, and the needle inches upward and upward until sixty-five jumps to seventy-five, then eighty-five. Surely you can outrun them. But when you look, they're moving in on you.

One takes the shape of the windshield. He has the face of the devil, at least what you think the devil would look like if you met up with him, and you believe you have. His face is directly in front of yours. You try to look through him to see the road.

He asks if you want to play a game of trivia. "If you win," he says, "I'll leave you alone. We'll all leave you alone." You say yes, because you're playing for sanity.

He says, "Name the seven deadly sins."

You know this one and recite quickly: "Lust, pride, anger, envy, sloth, greed, and gluttony."

"Very good. When does a town become a city?"

"When it has a cathedral," you say with a smile. Thank God for Agnes.

"One U.S. state that grows coffee."

"Hawaii," you scream, and clap your hands. You're on a roll. You'll beat him and get rid of this burden.

"How many cups of coffee does it take to kill the average human?"

You lift your travel mug, gulp and calculate at the same time. "In four hours' time, one hundred cups or ten grams."

"What is the gender of a clam?"

"A clam starts out as a male and some decide to become female." They metamorphose, you think. Too easy.

"What is the shortest verse in the bible?"

He's got you, but you don't let on. You pretend to think about it, like you really know anything about the bloody bible. Too much time passes. Sweat sprinkles your shirt like rain. Your truck feels like it's slowing because of the weight of the washers and dryers in the back.

"The answer," he demands.

"I don't know," you whisper, and his faces changes shape and color. His tongue lashes out like a snake's, and he hisses at you. Droplets of blood pop out of his pores and fizz as they make contact with oxygen.

"'Jesus wept.' John 11:35," he hisses. "JesusweptJesusweptJesusweptJesuswept."

Up ahead someone is waving. Your truck has already slowed to twenty, so you pull over and get out. You jog toward a four wheeler pressed, like an accordion, into the trunk of a tree. Just ahead a man is staggering toward you. One of his arms is missing. He's holding it in his other hand. You start to fall back but someone says, "Take me with you."

You hesitate before walking to the front of the car. A person, the passenger maybe? Her head is smashed between the bumper and the tree. Her skull is split like a seam. Her torso and legs are splayed front down, over the hood, and her feet are touching the wipers.

"Jesus!" you scream. "Oh Jesus!"

You bend to look through the driver's window and you can see the trunk of the tree.

Nailed to the bark is a photograph wrapped in plastic inside a heart. The picture is of a man and woman. You can identify them as the two here, now.

You back away.

"You fucker!" she yells at you. "Get me out of here."

You run back to your truck. In the pumping of your heart and the pounding of your feet against the pavement you hear it. It's the sound of Jesus weeping.

Two days later I find myself in South Carolina. I have no recollection of the drive or of delivering the washers and dryers. The rings around my eyes are so heavy, they feel bruised. As soon as Jesse sees me, he jumps off his stool and takes my bag.

"Come on, darlin'," he says softly, and leads me to his room. He steers me through the small living area, through the kitchenette and into the bathroom.

I smell so bad even I turn away from the stench. Jesse doesn't seem to notice. He puts warm water in a bowl and then asks me to strip. He stays behind me so he can't see, and washes my arms, back, and neck, then reaches around to wash my front. He dries me, then puts me in a T-shirt. His touch is as tender as a mother's. After he puts me in sweatpants, he guides me to the bed, pulls the covers down and tucks me in.

"I won't sleep," I say, feeling a tear fall down the side of my face. "I'm afraid."

"I'll sit right here, sugar," he assures me, and pulls a chair next to the headboard.

"What time is it?" I ask. My eyes are closed. I may already be asleep.

I hear him pull his pocket watch out. "Just after one."

"In the morning?"

"That's right."

"Will you wake me in time for the ten-thirty show?"

Jesse laughs kindly. "Twenty-one hours from now?" I nod. "We'll see," he says. "Now close your eyes. I'll watch over you."

"You've come from out of nowhere, Jesse Reid."

A soft laugh catches in his throat.

"Can I have my ocean rock?"

He looks through my jean pockets and then hands it to me. I sleep with it under the pillow.

It's eleven at night when I finally emerge from the room with Jesse. He didn't wake me in time for the show, but I heard a bar full of people singing. He takes me by the hand and leads me to the dance floor. Everyone stops to watch. You'd think that he's never taken a woman onto the dance floor before. No one else joins us, it's too monumental.

He doesn't hold me close; he keeps a safe distance between our bodies. But his body is there in front of me, tormenting me, testing to see if I'll make it through without collapsing into him and making him kiss me. Which, of course, probably won't happen because the dancing and hand holding has taken close to eight weeks to happen.

Jesse's voice fuses with Paul McCartney's and they sing about trouble and Mother Mary and words of wisdom, and somewhere in the lyrics Jesse says, "Tell me what happened. What's brought you to this point?"

"This story has already been told," I say without an ounce of intonation.

"That's what the surprise ending is for," Jesse teases lightly. His face seems so close to mine, while his body is still a million miles away.

"Even the surprise ending," I announce, just as flatly as before.

"Not our story," Jesse argues, but it's more like a whisper with conviction, and suddenly I feel the few whiskers on his chin pinprick my cheek. I think of my middle school boyfriends, when the stiff hair was trying to bully the baby hair out of the way, but the baby hair was obstinate, fighting for the land it occupied first.

Oh yes, I want to say, even our story has been told, you can't be so bold as to think it hasn't. But I'm unable to because I don't know why that exact thought has come into my head. It isn't as though we're really all that special or different. Jesse pulls me off the dance floor and gives a hand signal to Gary, as he leads me to the same place we've just come from.

Every last muscle in my body is flexed and ready for the force of his muscles and organs. I don't care if it's rough and quick, or soft and slow, I just want to feel something normal and I want to feel it from him. Yet, there's a nagging in the pit of my stomach, something that tells me the only thing that'll be operational tonight is my mouth and tongue as they throw words about Dennis and his life into a room inhabited by two people who, it seems, are unlikely to become lovers.

blueprint
inner information about a person's future

I tell Jesse that the story of Dennis—which, in turn, becomes the story of us—does not begin at his death in 1995 or even at the time when he and I first met in 1991. It goes back to 1960, the year of his birth and maybe even further, to the time in which his father's stubborn sperm managed to survive the long uphill trek to penetrate his mother's fleeing egg.

I tell Jesse that during all this—that is to say the moment the egg and sperm came into contact, the prenatal stage of development the core of Dennis Lutz's genetic blueprint came into being and changed the course of history before it was even able to play itself out.

Jesse says that my theory is debatable, but it's my story, so he lets it slide.

It's my belief that Dennis was born into bad luck. Even his name was proof of his misfortune. Dennis Lutz. "You know what his nickname was in high school!" I exclaim.

Jesse says, "That certainly is an interesting opinion, but don't you think you're stretching it a bit? Don't you think you need some solid proof to support your claim?"

I dig through my bag and pull out a cheap gold watch.

"I stole this," I confess in a conspiratorial whisper.

Jesse turns it over in his hands, unimpressed. "If you're going to take up theft, you may need some pointers. I, myself, am not well versed in thievery, but I can tell you that I'd look for jewelry that's a little more expensive than this."

I huff at him.

He laughs. If I were a poet like Shakespeare or Mr. Whitman, I'd say that sometimes when Jesse laughs, there's a sparkle in his eyes, like you see when the sun hits a glass prism. But the comparison is too ordinary, and besides, I'm not like either poet at all. I can't give words to Jesse's eyes but I know how they make me feel. His eyes give life to every organ inside me. A life filled with helium, and I rise above the ground when his eyes twinkle like that.

"I'm trying to tell you something," I say, not as meanly as I want it to sound because his eyes have taken away my anger.

"I know, darlin'. I'm sorry. Who'd you steal it from?"

"Dennis."

"That's kind of morbid, wouldn't you say?"

"Not from his dead body. He was the only one who had a watch on that day. I kept it. I didn't give it to the police."

"Help me along a little, Danny," Jesse says patiently.

"When I first came back to trucking last October, I took a run to Louisiana. One day I stopped—this is gonna sound stupid," I mumble.

Jesse lights a couple cigarettes, gets two beers out of the refrigerator, and sits next to me on the couch to knead the tension out of my shoulders. He has, over the past several weeks, stocked his tiny refrigerator with dark beer and chocolate bars, my two favorite foods. "I hit a pit stop that I'd heard a few truckers talking about because it has a psychic. The only thing I told her was that the watch wasn't mine. She took it from me, weighed it in her hands and then placed it on top of a deck of tarot cards. Then she dealt out several cards in what she called a luck spread. It's got six cards in the shape of an upside-down triangle. Three on top, two below, then one. Every time she turned a card over, she got this weird look on her face, like she was startled by it, like a doctor in horror movies when a demonic baby comes out of the mother."

"You make interesting analogies."

I smile.

"The first card was the Tower. Next to it was Eight of Swords, then The World Reversed. The second row was the Queen of Cups and Ten of Swords. The last, the Ace of Cups Reversed."

"Each card has a meaning, and each position means something, as does the way in which the cards work together. There're lots of factors here, Danny," Jesse cautions.

"Sure. Look, I wrote down what she said."

I dig through my bag for the notes.

"The first position in the luck spread is an overview for the luck factor. And in Dennis's case, it was the Tower. Shock, disruption, structural flaws, unavoidable change, collapse…"

"And the walls came a'tumbling down."

I drop my hands on the tablet and look up at him.

"You know, the Battle of Jericho."

I shake my head.

"The bible? Never mind, just go on."

"Second position says how the luck will affect your life. Eight of Swords, the figure is tied to a sword, blindfolded, surrounded by other swords. This is what the psychic said, 'A vicious circle, isolation, inability to move, disappointment, fear, limitation.' So far, two very negative cards." Jesse starts to challenge, but I hold my hand up to stop him. "Third position is the area where luck might appear. The World Reversed. The psychic said, 'Unfinished business, imperfection, frustration, obstacles, stubbornness.' The fourth card was who or what will enter your life as a result of luck. It's the Queen of Cups and it gives you the opportunity to examine your life. She said there's a choice based on sincere feelings, that the queen has a sixth sense, mystery, occult interests, prophecy. Based on that Dennis chose not to examine his life."

"But, Danny—" Jesse nearly pleads.

"I'm not finished," I say, speaking faster. "The Ten of Swords: the end of a cycle. Ruin, defeat, the death of something. This position is how the luck will help you attain what you desire. And last, Ace of Cups Reversed: no one loves me. Depression, separation, distress. Sex without love. That was him completely."

Jesse is visibly disturbed. His face is in his hands, he exhales loudly.

"Don't you see, Jesse," I appeal and grip his sleeve, "that everything about him was unlucky. As soon as he inherited that name, hell as soon as the sperm fertilized the egg, he became unlucky."

"Granted, I don't know much about tarot, but I was under the impression that in tarot the future isn't necessarily permanent, that the cards give hints to help move you toward a better future."

He's trying to deflate my balloon, but I'm stubborn. "Free will versus destiny? Dennis was destined to meet me; I don't care what anyone says. The Queen of Cups proves it. I was part of his bad luck. I was his death card. It was the beginning of the end when I walked into it."

Jesse sits forward and shakes his head. "Hold on, hold on. I think you're confusing the two. You're changing definitions to suit your need to prove you had something to do with his death. I can argue that the beginning of his death began the day he was born. Death is a part of our fate. Free will—"

"Don't give me that religious psycho-babble horseshit. His name proves it!" I holler, but I've lost sight of my points and my proof. I'm confused by all of it, by how I've gotten here, by why I'm forced to explain what's completely clear in my head to a man who isn't sexually attracted to me, who refuses to see beyond the obvious.

"Ten tarot readers could interpret that spread ten different ways," he says quietly.

"This makes sense. It makes sense in here," I whisper, pointing to my brain.

"Don't get angry, sugar. It's a little like trying to explain a dream, the way it loses its meaning, its color, its validity, as soon as you try to explain it."

We're sitting on the couch directly next to each other, not moving really except for our breathing. Yet Jesse slides closer to me. I'm beginning to break down because of it.

"Just forget it," I say quietly and light a cigarette from the one in my mouth.

"I don't want to forget it. I want us to understand each other. Let's just go back to what you said about his name. I'm assuming his nickname was Putz?"

Of course it was, I want to scream, but instead I nod.

"I fail to see how that one thing means he had an unlucky life. Surely even you had a bad day now and again during high school."

"Did you?"

"I didn't go to high school."

I'm a bad interviewer. Instead of jumping on his answer, and following a different question and answer track, one Jesse has kept off-limits, I stick to my imaginary script about Dennis and his bloody fucking bad luck life, and how it's gotten my life wrapped inside of his.

I'm suddenly wild with anxiety. I'm chain smoking and drinking shots of Jack as though they're thimbles of water. He's asked the question and now I have to share my life, maybe even understand it a little. I've managed to stay clean from my high school life for over twelve years, and here Jesse Reid is pushing me off my sobriety wagon.

Life in high school boiled down to two things, I tell him: categories and classifications. They were pleasing to me in only one small way, we weren't unlike cars. Category: Ford, Classification: Mustang; Category: Ford, Classification: Festiva. It was better to own one than another, just like it was better to belong to one than the other. I knew I wasn't the only misfit, and it seemed logical that I should have found comfort in other kids' misfortunes. But I wasn't like the rest of them. I didn't want to be someone's second choice, nor did I want to be stuck with someone else's sloppy seconds. So, for better or worse, I chose solidarity rather than friendship with girls and boys I'm sure had more to offer than the popular kids.

That was bad, but knowing I wasn't good at anything was worse.

Home economics, basketball, cheerleading. No one had to tell me I looked out of place because I felt it. I wasn't built right to be a cheerleader, and the teachers tried to be more sensitive than the girls who put it bluntly; my boobs were too small. They stuck theirs out to show me what a real set was supposed to look like. I heard one basketball coach say to another, "With long legs like those…what a waste." And as far as home ec went, I was more help changing the compressor on the refrigerator than I was mixing ingredients.

But I found a home when I was asked by the home ec teacher to deliver a note to the automotive teacher.

"How can I describe it," I say to Jesse. I know I must look wistful because that's how I feel.

"It was as enchanting for you to stand there and watch him build an engine as it would have been for an amateur artist to walk into a room where Van Gogh was painting *The Starry Night*."

"Would that be a big deal?" I ask stupidly.

"Very big," Jesse tells me with a smile.

I found a home but I was still ignored, at least until three girls in my class were stranded on the side of the road with a flat tire. Most of me wanted to keep driving, let them struggle, break their nails, dirty their clothes. Of course, I didn't. I made a U-turn and changed the flat in no time, finding some pleasure in rolling the lug nuts swiftly and expertly. They watched my hands—the short, oil-stained nails, the tear in the knuckle from where a wrench had skipped over a stripped bolt—work with as much ease and skill of a surgeon. Three faces twisted in confusion and discomfort, and maybe a teeny tiny bit of gratitude and wonderment. I wiped my hands on my jeans, tossed the flat in the trunk with the jack, and got in my dad's pickmeup without so much as a thank you from any of them.

I wasn't ignored anymore, I was pointed to and giggled at.

My first real job after high school was at Bill Rae's Auto Repair. I made everyone uneasy. Bill hinted that I stay "busy" behind a hood or beneath the body until people got used to me being there. I understood that he didn't want me showing my face. When I sat down at the lunch table with two other mechanics, both of them packed up their lunches and left the table. The second day Bill asked me to wait until they were finished because it wouldn't look good if all the mechanics were on break at once. The third day Bill asked me if I minded staying back by the employee rest room because it made customers uncomfortable seeing a girl eating lunch while wearing greasy coveralls. Instead, I sat on the counter in the women's room, my ass hanging over the sink. I stopped bringing lunch after that. I left the shop and walked down a path through a wooded area behind the garage, sat by the creek, smoked, and thought to myself, I've found something I'm good at, so why don't I belong?

Three weeks into the job, I was still only changing oil and headlights and flats. I was itching to get my hands dirty, to show Bill I knew what I was doing. Eventually, I did get my chance, because we were backed up. An automatic transmission burned up and the owner, despite my repeated warning, decided to get a used transmission from a junk yard. I reluctantly put it in and less than a week later, the valve body leaked and the transmission puked all over again. It was exactly what they were looking for and I got canned.

"So, yes," I tell Jesse, "I had a bad day, or two, or four years." I did have a couple friends, went on enough dates, but I was lonely a lot of the time. My father wasn't around as much as I wanted him to be. He was the person who understood me the best of all, but when he left on a run, I understood. All these things made for not the happiest teenage years but when it came to genetic blueprints, Danny Fletcher's and Dennis Lutz's weren't even comparable.

the natural direction of time's arrow

*time moves forward in the direction of statistically prevailing disorder,
therefore, things age*

I stood inside Dennis's apartment, mesmerized.

I felt him around me. His spirit had formed into an airtight drum that was smothering me. I wasn't exactly sure how to conserve the little oxygen I had so I did the only thing I could think of. I took a deep breath and held it for as long as I could, then studied my surroundings.

I had come to deliver the belongings from Dennis's locker. My plan was to drop the bag and go, but now I couldn't move. The Dennis in the duffle was no more likable than the Dennis surrounding me. One thing was certain, you wouldn't know Dennis was dead. Everything was still operative and on-call. There was no sign that things in the apartment hadn't been touched in three weeks. Every room was visible from where I stood and, aside from an absurd number of ticking clocks everywhere, the motif was obscene and reckless. At first, I admit, it was arousing, but then what I was seeing really hit me.

Hot plate, TV, Vacuum, Mattress, Seatless chair, Fridge, Fork, Knife, Photos, Dish, Desk, Couch, Chains, Leashes, Leather, Porn, Pillows, Whips, Posters, Pots, Pans, Handcuffs, Step stool, Rope, Bondage, Ass plugs, Spoons, Bowls, Videos, Microwave, Hood, Collar, Cock harness, Nipple clamps, Extenders, Rings, Submission, Anger, Aggression, Restraints, Domination, Violence, RageForceFucking Everywhere.

Dennis was gone. He wasn't missed, so you'd think it would've been easy to stop looking around at his apartment because it was just like his locker. There had been two *Playboy* centerfolds stuck to it and smack dab in the middle of them was a round yellow "Don't Worry, Be Happy" smiley face stick. A few weeks after his funeral, a small group of us had sat on the bench and emptied his locker together. We took turns pulling stuff out because none of us wanted the job to begin with. Porn movies, dirty magazines, condoms. There was a pattern here. Polaroids of nude women in compromising positions. Real photographs, ones he took. In one we could see his image in a mirror, holding the camera. His naked ass, his penis sticking out, the skin from his gut sagging like an oversized water balloon.

"What the..." Pip had said with amazed disgust. "How did he find women to sleep with him?"

"You do," I needled, as we studied the picture. Pip and I had that give-and-take teasing.

"I'm not a freak."

We dropped the stuff in a duffel using two fingers, like prongs, as though it were contaminated.

"What're we going to do with this?" Neil asked.

"Danny can drop it by his place on her way home," Pip retaliated with a smile.

"Why don't you do it?" I asked.

"Because you're the boss."

One of the many perks. Seemed highly unfair, but I wasn't going to fight it. It was the least I could do.

Fortunately, at his funeral, he didn't have an open casket. Every one of us was thankful. We were the only ones there. Since no family members showed up, we assumed he didn't have any. Even among us he didn't have a single friend, so we felt obligated to stay to the end to stare at his coffin and try to recall good memories. The preacher asked us to. Not a one of us could think of anything. We whispered that fact to each other. I think Neil started it. He whispered to Buzz, "What are you thinking about?" hoping he'd share. Buzz shrugged, at a loss. Then Neil asked Pip, and Pip asked Vic, and so on. We sat there like unprepared high school students, hoping someone would let us copy their homework. Eventually Buzz turned to me. All the guys were listening when he whispered, "What are you thinking about, Danny?" I was their last hope, as sad as that was, but I wasn't sure I wanted to share my memory, because it wasn't good. But it was Buzz and the guys, so I did. I said, "Two six nine." Everyone sank back in their folding chairs and ran with it.

Dennis and I had never been on friendly terms. He came on to me my third day on the job. It's only fair to admit that Pip did too. But they went about it differently. Most men are shy around me. One former boyfriend said it was because I'm tall, another, because I have a look that says, I'm not interested. Whenever I went out at night, I made a concerted effort to soften that look. But not at work. There I wanted to be taken seriously. I knew I'd have to prove myself, so sleeping with the day help wouldn't benefit me.

Pip is a handsome guy. Short and muscular, but not my type. When he asked me out to dinner, I let him down easy. I told him that, though I thought he was good looking, I was already with someone else, which was true.

Now Dennis, he was different. Dennis rode the bus line after work some nights and would pass a folded piece of paper to women as he was exiting. He walked past my truck my third day as I was leaving work and handed me mine. It always said the same thing. I know this because I met a couple women who were approached on the bus. This was Dennis's business card:

For $5 I'll eat your pussy for as long as you want.

He was watching me from the bus stop, perhaps expecting a nod. As soon as I read his note, I crumpled it in my fist and marched toward the stop where he stood with four other people. The bus was taking its first turn toward them. And here I was, on the street, in the middle of another word problem.

A bus with fifteen passengers on board is heading south in traffic, traveling thirty-five miles per hour toward its destination. At the same time an enraged woman carrying a crumpled piece of paper nearly the same weight in insinuation as all the passengers on the bus, is running ten miles per hour toward the same destination. Who will get there first?

I did, of course, because I had more at stake. I grabbed him by his shirt collar and shoved the piece of paper into his mouth. "That's the only thing you'll ever eat from me," I snarled. I pissed him off good. Half the guys from our shift had watched me run across the parking lot and hurdle the park benches. Not bad for a woman who smoked a pack a day.

A couple days later I was riding the roller, machine two six nine, with Buzz. He was loosening the muscle in my neck while I was driving. We passed the gang truck where Dennis and a couple college kids were waiting, and he screamed loud enough for everyone to hear over the rumbling of the machine, "Don't bother, Buzz. She goes for girls."

I parked the machine and as graceful as any ballerina in work boots, jumped to the ground and then climbed up the back of the gang truck with one hop. I stood in the doorway of the back cab. I said, "Does someone here have something they'd like to say?" I'm normally a nonviolent person unless I'm pushed. The part-time kids dropped their heads. I stood there with my hands dug into my hips, in the late afternoon sun, all greased with oil and sweat, making my tan look like dirt. Dennis wasn't afraid of me. He stood up, trying to tower over me, but he was pear shaped and a sloucher, so we were nearly eye to eye. His bangs were in his eyes, and he said, "You walk around here like you got a stick shoved up your ass. You think you're too goddamned good for everyone, and all you are is a worthless tar baby like the rest of these assholes who can't get any other job. You got no brains, no life, and not a ounce of feminine quality."

I couldn't think of an appropriate comeback because I didn't even know that a tar baby was a name for someone who worked on an oiling crew, and I was standing there smelling like oil and sweat, looking like a woman without an ounce of feminine quality. Dennis walked toward me, backing me into the sun. My hands had curled into fists against my hips, and I stood ready to throw a punch to show him just how much feminine quality I had, when I felt Buzz's palm on my arm.

"Let's get going, Danny," Buzz said.

I popped a cigarette in my mouth and chewed the end.

I said to Dennis with the confidence of a fortune teller, "It's just a matter of time."

Time. Had time been the blame for Dennis's death? If I had stayed on my machine ten seconds longer, I reasoned, Dennis wouldn't have had the opportunity to get on it. The chipper stopped because there was seven feet of oiled road that didn't have rock. Buzz had told me they were waving all the trucks backward so they could drop the chips. Instead of waiting ten more seconds, I jumped down because I thought the chipper was broken. It all boiled down to ten seconds. A thought. A decision. Time: it was my first experience with it stopping.

I lived through Dennis's death as though I were moving through quicksand, but when time went back to normal, I still had to fill in the missing pieces. Buzz, Pip, and the guys gave me some answers, and the newspapers did too. Moments of time lost to me came back when I read the misleading articles. I'd read a false fact and say to myself, No, no that's not what happened. It happened like this.

There are an estimated fifty-eight days of sunshine in Central New York. We couldn't oil the roads if it was raining or, consequently, if the roads were wet. August 10 was destined to be a hot, humid, sunny day. Other than that, its only other noteworthy events were observed by individuals, not by the nation, let alone the world. For example, there were no serial killers on the loose, or major sporting event upsets. Instead, on that day in our region, a total of twelve babies would be born. Twenty-two people would die. A teenage boy would save an eight-year-old from drowning. There would be a BBQ picnic and as a result, six people would have extreme cases of diarrhea. And there would be Dennis.

We had already finished our breakfasts and were heading to the job site. Pip was driving the gang truck and I was next to him in the passenger seat. Ed, Pete, the college kids, and Dennis were in the back compartment, completely shut off from us.

I was chain smoking because I'd let Dennis get to me. Pip kept glancing my way. If Buzz were with us, he'd broach the subject. He'd say, "You deserve the aggravation because you let him get to you." But Pip, knowing I'd eventually say something, waited for me to speak.

"Stupid goddamn fucking fucker of a fuck."

"Creative," he mumbled. "You know, he knows it gets to you."

He meant about Dennis and his stories about fucking. We had five college workers, three males, two females. Even though he was twenty years older than the college kids, and uncouth, and from a different social class, Dennis was the leader of their pack. They hovered around him like disciples. Most days two would call in sick or go on a short vacation—one was Shari Eliot, who stopped coming in all together. I thought I knew why. Though I had no proof, I suspected Dennis had taken advantage of her in the salt shed. With her gone, we were left with only four workers, which wasn't enough. Unless we counted Dennis, and none of us did.

Of the group who were left, Donna liked talking about sex. She gave the others a commentary every morning on which section of the grocery store she and her boyfriend had done it in, and how. Dennis encouraged the stories, even though the rest of us told her to exercise a little modesty. She listened to Dennis. While we sat at the diner, trying to eat our breakfasts, Donna put on makeup, fluffed her hair, and told her stories. It got Dennis going. He asked her questions and her answers gave him fantasies to get off on for the whole day, and she knew it. In the middle of breakfast on August 10, they sat across the table from each other, so the whole restaurant heard their conversation. It was no accident.

"Did you sit on his face?" Dennis asked and looked at me, waiting for me to respond.

"Of course," she answered.

"You wanna sit on mine?"

The dumb bitch giggled. Disgusted, I stood and fished

singles out of my pocket, then quietly apologized to our waitress. The others followed suit, and we filed out, fanning out to our apparatuses.

The only thing more offensive than them was the heat. It was already ninety-four degrees, and the humidity was one hundred percent suffocating.

By 8:15, I was chain smoking, Pip was watching me with concern, and Buzz and the other guys were in their dump trucks, hauling stone to Bishop Road. The payloader, which would play a very important role in our lives in another hour, was being driven in the opposite direction to a different job site.

Pip pulled into the parking lot of the church on Bishop Road, where the roller and chipper were parked. One of the men from upstairs was sitting in a county car waiting for us. I picked up my hard hat and used it to bang on the Plexiglas separating the cab from the back of the gang truck. Ed and Pete saw me hold it up, and put theirs on as soon as they jumped off the bed. I adjusted the inside setting of mine, and reluctantly put it on.

I got out of the truck at the same time Jerry White got out of his car—with his hard hat on. Ed and Pete ignored us and went to start up the chipper and the roller. Pip drove the gang truck out of the parking lot before he got roped in. They all left me to stand alone, chicken shits.

"Jerry," I said.

"Danny."

"I'm surprised to see you out here."

Jerry nodded and loosened his tie. "Goddamn it's hot."

This is only beginning, I wanted to tell him, stick around for the oil. As soon as he departed, my T-shirt would be off, and I'd be riding around in a thinning, tar-stained undershirt, we all would. It was a small tactic toward surviving the heat.

"I got a phone call yesterday," he said.

"A phone call, or someone was out spying on us?"

"Listen, Danny, it's not me."

"No, I suppose it isn't. After all, you were one of us once.

Now you just sit and take it quietly up the ass from the guys downtown. Never pegged you for the type, but hey, we all have our secrets."

"Don't get too mouthy, Danny. One word from me, and you'll be scooping shit out of the sewers."

He was being an asshole, but I laughed a little.

"Okay," I said, taking a drag of a cigarette. "You're here because one of your spies ratted us out, not because I called yesterday and told your secretary that this road is too fucking soft to oil. As you can see, all the kids are in work boots and wearing their hard hats when they're on the road."

"What about flags and vests?"

"They're completely black with tar. We need new ones. We have no walkie-talkies. I put the paperwork in weeks ago."

"And the full timers?" he asked, ignoring the statement.

"Ed and Pip wear theirs when they're on the chipper. Buzz and them are in their trucks."

"I guess I'm talking about you, Danny? How many times do you need to be told to wear your hard hat?"

I kicked a rock with the side of my boot. I knew it was going to come down to me.

"It's on my head, isn't it?"

"I don't mean just carrying it with you on the machines. I mean it stays on your head. If that's too difficult to remember, maybe we can get you a position in the offices with the other women."

I laughed as if to mock him.

"And what about Denny?" he continued.

"Dennis is your problem. He never listens to anything I say."

"It's your job to make him listen," he said, challenging me a little more. Once you stripped him of his shirt and tie, he was still a good old boy who didn't want women on the job.

"Fuck you, Jerry. It's goes way beyond that. Why the hell do you think those kids don't listen? He tells them it's okay to go on vacation, he tells them to take breaks. He totally undermines everything you or I say. All I've got is Donna out there flagging, and most of the time she's bitching that her fucking hair's going flat, and her makeup's running, and she has to pee, and her fucking feet hurt, and all this other bullshit that no one wants to listen to. Traffic gets bad so I had to put one of the guys on with her—"

"Where's the other girl?"

"Jesus Christ, I've already told you twice that she doesn't come in anymore, Jerry. I have to shuffle everyone around. Now I've only got two guys shoveling. I left the chipper to drive the roller so there's just Ed and Pip on the chipper and Pete's driving the gang truck."

"What's Dennis doing?"

"Nothing. He doesn't get off his lazy fat ass and do a thing, unless of course Donna shows him her tits, then he'll take over for a while. It's like working with perverted adolescents."

"Put Denny on the roller."

"No chance in hell. Definitely not on this road. This road should be blacktopped. These trucks are too heavy for this road, Jerry. Last year we did the same thing on Parker Road, and because of the high volume of traffic we had three accidents. On top of that, I'm shorthanded."

"Then put Denny on the roller," he repeated.

"I don't trust Dennis with anything bigger than a shovel. I want him off this shift."

"Can't happen. Union'll be all over my ass," Jerry said, turning to go.

"I can give you something to work with."

Now he looked back at me. "Is there some kind of trouble going on? Tell me now, Danny, or else I'm done with this conversation."

I only had what I'd seen, and that could be construed two different ways. He'd had her by the wrists and was pulling her playfully toward the gang truck that was parked in the salt shed. She seemed to be resisting, but not with enough urgency to make me do something. She stopped coming to work after that. When she came in to pick up her last paycheck, I asked her if she was coming back, but she looked away and practically ran out of the bay.

I took my hard hat off and scratched my head. As much as I believed he raped her, there was no solid evidence and I knew it. Jerry turned again and walked toward his car.

"What about the road, Jerry? It's too soft to oil, it needs to be blacktopped."

"It's a secondary road, and secondary roads are oiled."

"It's gonna catch up to you, Jerry."

Jerry waved, amused, unmoved, and got into his nice, cool air-conditioned car.

There's nothing like watching a true convoy traveling a highway, particularly at night. The long-nosed diesels are all decked out, with extra lights on the cabs and trailers. People actually get excited to see us. It's like watching a parade drive by, a truly handsome sight, overwhelming even, because of the size and length and the fact that we drivers take pride in our rigs, and that we keep the American economy moving. What we can state that no one else can is that everything on you, in you, and around you came from us. We make a difference.

Our sad little county parade of trucks, though, was so amateurish it was more like a *Peanuts* cartoon. Everyday a piece of equipment broke down (usually the chipper), and the repair was always half-assed. When we had enough workers, we were led by a flagger, followed by an 18 wheel Mack truck that sprayed oil out of a squeegee the length of the bumper. About twenty feet behind the oiler was the chipper, or chip spreader, that dropped stone out of a bucket onto the hot oil as it moved slowly forward. The dump trucks had the hardest job. They had to drive backward, opposite traffic, and connect to the back of the chipper. The drivers had to watch in their side mirrors for someone on the chipper, Pip in our case, to direct when to lift and lower their boxes with his thumb, especially around power lines. The stone poured out of the boxes and down two conveyer belts that fed into the front bucket of the chipper.

Once the truck was out of stone, it pulled away and the next truck would do the same thing. A little ways behind the dump truck was the gang truck where Dennis and the two college guys sat, backs to the trucks ahead, legs dangling off the bed, work boots swinging with every bump the truck hit. Donna walked alongside the gang truck, swinging her flag like a baton, as though she were an eight-year-old girl working toward majorette. The roller was the last truck in line, directly behind the gang truck. I sat on top of it, watching Dennis, Donna, and the two other guys who had the shovel and rake between them waiting for piles of stone to fall.

At 8:30 a.m. the sun was blazing orange-red and the tar on the road bubbled like hot water on a stove. Thick and spicy, it was gearing up to clog our pores. As we slowly moved forward, sweat formed above my hairline, then trickled down the sides of my face, stopping for a second on my cheekbones before continuing down to my neck. The hot steam from the oil drifted in the air, reaching us in the form of a white fog. There was no breeze; we were barely moving.

I was seriously beginning to regret having taken this job.

The line of trucks continued forward, but the gang truck stopped after it passed over a huge pile of stones. The roller, an 18,000-pound rectangular vehicle filled with water to give it the weight to crush the stone into the oil, swayed unsteadily over large piles, due to the eight thin rubber tires across the front and eight across the back. The machine would have been safer if it had a cage around the steering mechanism. But this was the county we were talking about, and all our machines were old and on their last legs.

When we stopped to rake the piles, I yelled down from the roller for someone to give me a watch because I'd forgotten mine. Everyone ignored me.

"Let me make this a little clearer," I yelled again. At some point during these past couple of years, I had turned into a miserable bitch. "If I don't have a watch, you don't get a lunch break."

Donna walked over to Dennis, took the watch off his arm, and brought it over to me.

"Thank you," I said. She gave me a fake smile and went back to twirling her flag.

The two college guys, Ernie and Ken, were trying to size down the pile of stone. Dennis remained sitting on the bed of the gang truck, watching Donna. Our line of trucks was now twenty feet ahead, which meant that the oil would dry before I had a chance to drive over the stone with the roller. I jumped off the roller and marched angrily toward the gang truck.

"Get off your ass, Dennis, and help the guys shovel this down," I yelled. "Useless bastard couldn't pour piss out of his own boot if the instructions were written on the bottom," I mumbled to myself.

Dennis picked up a shovel and threw it at my feet. It landed with a dull ring.

"You do it, princess."

"You're done, Dennis. The union won't support you when I give them the details of your salt-shed outing."

"Sorry, princess, I don't know what you're talking about."

"I'm blowing you in this afternoon."

"I'd like you to blow me," he said, puckering his lips into a kiss. The thing was, there was no smile on his face.

When I picked up the shovel, I refrained from bashing his head in, and helped level the rock instead. Once we got it leveled, we quickly moved the gang truck and roller forward until we caught up to the dump trucks. Everything stopped again. When I heard the gang truck turn off, I figured we were stopped because of a broken machine, probably the chipper that was four trucks ahead of us. I did the same, turned off the roller, and lit a cigarette. Both the gang truck and the roller were parallel to the ditch, but the roller was dangerously close to the edge. As I was about to turn my machine back on to move it, Donna hollered from the center of the road, "What time is it?"

I looked at the watch and said, "It's 8:50."

"Fuck, man," Ken said and lay back on the floor of the gang truck. He covered his face from the sun with a sweatshirt.

"It's going to be the longest fucking day of my life," Dennis said. "I shouldn't've bothered coming."

I wanted to let fly with a nice sarcastic comeback like, And yes, how we would have suffered without you, but it was too hot.

Moaning, Ken jumped down while Donna climbed onto the gang truck and moved into the shelter, out of the sun. No one said a word; everyone moved cautiously, using no extra effort, to conserve any last bit of cool air in our bodies. Everyone concentrated on making a breeze blow. Ken joined Ernie and sat under a tree while Dennis followed Donna into the back cover of the gang truck, even though it would be like a sauna in there. I took off my hard hat, and lifted my undershirt so my stomach was bare, trying to give myself a little relief from the heat.

You don't focus in heat like that. You don't focus because you don't care, unless someone gives you something to care about. Donna did, when she playfully squealed and said, "No Dennis," I sat upright in my seat, and squinted to see into the gang truck, but the angle I was at, and the sun, made it difficult to do. Stealthily I jumped off the roller and moved toward the truck, climbing the steps without making a sound. I peered into the doorway and saw Donna standing with her back to the door, and Dennis sitting in front of her. They didn't hear me, they weren't even paying attention because Dennis was finger fucking her with one hand, while jerking off with the other. A nice little activity to make the time go by more quickly.

"Un-fucking-believable," I barked, startling them.

Donna pulled the zipper of her jeans up, but Dennis apparently found it all very exciting, and kept everything out in the open.

"I'm taking you back to the shop during lunch break," I said to her. "You're fired."

"You can't fire me."

"I can't? I just did. Get out of here. Go wait with the guys."

I turned and watched her go. As soon as she jumped down

from the gang truck, I felt him behind me, pushing into me, pressing his dick against my back.

"Sure you wouldn't like to give it a try? With a man, I mean," he said.

I turned to face him, then looked down at his cock and gave a half laugh. "Find me a man first. Now back off before you're sorry you ever started with me."

He did back off as he zipped his pants up, but he was pissed.

"Dyke," he whispered. I could smell the mix of body odor and dirt coming off him, or maybe it was me, who knew. He said it again, in case I didn't get it the first time. "Whoring dyke," he mumbled, before pushing past me, and spitting on the floor at my feet. He exited through the door leading to the back bed.

Shaking, I dug into my pockets for my pack of cigarettes, forgetting about the one I'd just pulled out, now crumpled in my hand. I wiped my hand against my pant leg, trying to get the tobacco flakes off my sweaty palm. Once again, I watched through the doorway as Dennis walked over to where Donna sat. She had climbed up onto the roller, like a child climbing up a tree after being scolded. She was sitting with her legs hanging off the side, crying.

Stupid, dumb young bitch, I thought. You deserve it for using such bad judgment. I jumped off the gang truck and stood in the space between it and the roller. There were tools, people, and trucks all around, but I noticed only Dennis standing on the road beside my machine. He flipped me off. His other hand held Donna's ankle.

If I wouldn't get fired, I thought to myself, I'd punch your fucking lights out.

His eyes peered at me with a hint of humor, like he heard me, like he knew I was too cowardly to do such a thing. Dismissing me with a wave, he climbed up the back of the roller. Before I did something that would get me into trouble, I decided to walk up the line of trucks to see what happened to the chipper. I remember because there was finally a breeze. A breeze. And for one second that made everything okay.

I continued forward but the sound of the back-up beeper, as it echoed over the rumble of the roller, stopped me in my tracks. I knew he was moving it just to piss me off, why else would he exert himself? I turned to look and Dennis flipped me off again. He looked over his left shoulder, instead of his right which was closest to the ditch, but could only see the end of the roller. He was too high up to see the ground.

"Stop the machine!" I hollered, as the roller crept closer to the ditch. Nobody on earth could hear me over that goddamned back-up beeper so it was safe to say, "You're a stupid bastard."

I looked from Dennis to the tires, from him to the ditch, then back to him. I started to wave my arms to warn him, started screaming his name to warn him, as the rubber tires inched slowly down the side of the embankment.

"Dennis!" I yelled, and looked for the others, but no one else seemed to understand what was happening.

That very second, I thought maybe he heard me because his eyes met mine, but maybe he just realized what was happening on his own. He turned the wheel as if to steer out of the ditch, to save the machine, or to save his own ass, and ultimately mine, from the trouble we'd both get in because of his stupidity. But everything was lost in the sound of the machine.

It was impossible that time could move so slowly, that every second felt like a lifetime. Dennis had time to react. I saw his hand on Donna's shoulder, pushing her off the roller. When he jumped from his seat, he looked like a long-distance runner in the air, his right leg bent, his left extended out behind him in a runner's start. But he was no runner. The ball of his right foot hit the top of the ditch, but he slid back down before he could pull himself up to the road itself. At the same moment, the bottom of the roller pitched, teetering up on one side and coming back down on top of him. Everything was lost in the sound of his scream, or maybe it was mine.

The truth was hard to accept, mostly because I had prided myself on hating Dennis. But unless you're born a murderer, hating someone and standing back to watch them die are two different things. After the roller tipped into the ditch, I ran like hell down the line of trucks, shouting for someone to call for an ambulance. Then I ran just as fast back to the ditch where Donna was petting Dennis's head and yowling like a cat.

"Donna!" I called. "Pull yourself together. You need to flag the traffic out of here."

"This is your fault! It's your machine. You made him do it!" she bellowed at me.

I didn't have time for this. Dennis's face was impacted into the ground. I leapt with one hop into the gang truck and grabbed the first item of clothing I could find, a blue hooded sweatshirt, and jumped back down again. Two more steps put me in the ditch with him. I tried to wedge the sweatshirt beneath his cheek, but there was very little room. He was pinned from the shoulder blades down. His knee was popped out and parallel to his chest. Welts and streaks of blood covered his now bare back. I lay next to him by pulling my legs up. He always wanted to be face-to-face with me, what a hell of a way to achieve it. I stuck my fingers into his mouth and pulled out stones and teeth and blood.

Everything in the air was still, except for the wheezing that came from his lungs. It sounded as though air was being let out of a balloon. I closed my eyes and moved as close as I could until my lips touched his. They were slippery with blood and salty from sweat, or maybe it was the other way around. When I pinched his nose to give him mouth to mouth, it squished and moved to the side. I dry heaved in his face but made myself calm down.

"Don't do this to me, Dennis. Not like this, you fucker. You're too fucking mean to die."

His lungs wheezed in reply. I thought that maybe, just maybe, he was trying to talk back.

I caressed his hair. "The payloader's on its way to pull this off you. Just hold on till then."

What was going on around me? Sirens, wind from propellers,

and people looking at us. "You take it easy, I can breathe for both of us," I told him, taking long gasping breaths.

I was breathing as if I had just been born, full and quick, until I couldn't feel the stinging of my heart nor the weight of the other organs in my body. The world around me was spinning fast, moving all about me like I was outside its gravitational force. In the background I could hear Donna still screaming, someone hollering for the ambulance, someone else throwing up, while Dennis was wheezing and gurgling, whispering all his secrets to me. I put one arm around his shoulder, the other around the top his head, my lips against his, and then closed my eyes. Together we listened to a bird sing in a tree. Together we lifted above our bodies and floated through the rays of the sun. It wasn't as hot where we were. We could hear and see everything. Dennis stood over us back down on the ground, then knelt beside me. I watched this from the sky. Someone put a hand on my shoulder and said, "Do the right thing, Danny. Go back." It sounded like Bobby.

I was roused as bits of gravel lashed my face. I looked up at the propellers of the Medevac above me. Dennis was inside the helicopter. I was lying in the middle of the road. I pushed myself up, feeling the stones under my hands, and waited until I had my bearings. Everyone moved around me as if I were invisible.

Some say he was crushed the second the roller hit him; others say he drowned in his own blood. Everyone agreed he was better off dead. They said he didn't feel a thing, but I think differently. He must have felt it hit him. I heard his scream. But maybe it was mine. It took the payloader nearly forty-five minutes to get there and once it finally did, it lifted the roller off Dennis and then Buzz lifted me out of the ditch. He said I wouldn't let go of Dennis's body.

When Dennis died, I heard a sound, and then in a matter of seconds shit hit the fan, but then I heard it again, and for the first time I heard the sound of the sky talking to me. Floating in the middle of it, wrapped in the center of it, I learned that the sky not only has a very distinct voice, but it has a lot to say.

It told me I would never go back to county work. I would use the insurance money from my parents' deaths and buy a truck, I would find someone to live in Agnes's garage, someone I could trust to take care of her because, like it or not, she was all I had. It told me that I'd dream about a blackness that was so dark, it would turn me inside out, it would make me feel as though in the end it would devour my soul. I'd go back on the road and see things that couldn't possibly be real. I would drive until the ticking stopped. Everything changed when the sky talked, and time started again. I changed, the world as I once knew it changed.

The bag with Dennis's belongings slipped from my hand. The ten-pound dumbbell at the bottom hit my boot. I would wonder, in a day or two, how my foot got bruised, but at the moment, it made me aware that I had control of the bones and ligaments in my body.

I got out as fast as I could.

Just like that day, I left Dennis's apartment a different person.

persistence
tendency for weather episodes to continue for some period of time

Winter in Central New York is notorious for being blustery, snowy, bitter cold. The winter before Dennis died, we had a five day stretch of lake effect snowstorms. Out of all the towns upstate, ours seemed to be the weakling on the playground. We were pushed and taunted from every angle, though Lake Ontario led the pack. The weathermen on the local channels were practically slap happy. We had snow needles, dendrites, even plates, although we needed a temperature close to minus thirty before the columns would come out. Watching columns fall from the sky, it was said, was like watching the cavalry come at you at full gallop. As we waited for columns to attack, I sat in the truck and conjured up hexagonal graph-like computer images dropping toward the ground. Then I started to draw them. Then I began to pray for them as much as the meteorologists. It gave me something to hope for.

By the end of the fourth day, we were a desert of white. Snow was falling about eight inches an hour. We ran out of places to push it. In some areas the piles were so high, the peaks reached the top of streetlamps. Schools were closed, and only essential government employees were made to go to work. We were on the roads twenty-four-seven. As if the fatigue and cold weren't difficult enough to battle, we had to veer around kids on sleds and adults on snowmobiles too.

But the extra cash didn't hurt. The city had to pay us over ten thousand dollars for over four hundred hours of overtime. I worked so much because I had no desire to sit alone in a garage apartment watching Agnes stroke Horace as she watched daytime dramas. She was really into soap operas but she complained because the women were too liberal, in and out of bed.

Sometimes I imagined what she was like as a young housewife and mother, her husband and son, sitting around the dinner table, napkins in laps, hands folded politely, good china and
suitable flatware laid out pretty, while she spooned vegetables
and meatloaf onto their plates. She described it clearly, and I
could see her watching intently while her husband sampled the
dinner, and then nodded approvingly before she was allowed
to sit down to eat. Over the years, as her son grew older, she'd
have to wait for him to do the same thing. Agnes told me there
were times she'd have to make another meal for the boy because
he didn't like the way it tasted during the taste test.

I said something like, "You should have made him get off
his lazy carcass and cook it himself."

"Oh," she said with feeble reason, "you know how teenage
boys are."

Excuses, I thought.

All those extra meals and he rarely called to see how she
was now. Not that I had been the ideal child. But I had always
called home every other day when I was out on the roads.
My mother never had much to say, but it eased her nerves
knowing I was all right. As soon as my dispatcher called and
told me about their accident, I turned around and was home
within twelve hours. And unlike Agnes's son, who only called
once when she was in the hospital with pneumonia, I was at
her bedside listening to her complaints and insults from the
moment I got out of work until visiting hours were over. Every night I let her offend my lifestyle, my friends, my clothes.
Every day I thought up snide comments that I knew would
give her enough to take off on. Comments about gender usually got her riled the most. I'd say things like, men should have
to cook instead of women, or women should be making the
same amount of money as men, or women should be able to
test out several sexual partners before settling down with one,
if at all. That one got her the most fired up. Usually, it would
keep her occupied until I left.

Even though he'd be sitting next to me in the rig, sometimes I thought about Buzz's home life. I'd eaten dinner with his family many times so I knew the routine. Everything was equal in his house. You scooped and passed from both sides. No one put napkins in laps. Sometimes we used plastic because no one felt like washing the dishes afterward. It wouldn't have crossed Deena's mind to stand there and wait to eat. The only time she ever did that was when the kids were babies, and even then, she and Buzz took turns feeding them. The racket during dinner was amazing. There were times, when neither parent was looking, when the boys would throw food at each other from across the table. Once, the baby was hit with a wad of scalloped potatoes, and I had to put my beer bottle to my lips so they couldn't see me smile. Once in a while, Buzz sent them to their rooms without dinner. But they kept stashes of Halloween candy hidden in their closets. They didn't know that we knew, they thought they were sneaky, so we had a momentary adult laugh. It was nice to be part of a nonviolent conspiracy.

Most of the time everyone at Buzz and Deena's table talked at once. It was like our crew breakfasts at work. We always ate at the same diner, sat at the same tables, and ordered the same foods. When we walked in, the waitress waved, and had put in our orders by the time she brought us coffee. We were on county time, after all. Buzz, Pip, Russ, and I sat at a booth. Vic, Ed, Neil, and Pete sat at the table next to us. During the summer Dennis chose to sit with the college kids instead of the table with the others. He was always on the prowl.

Any one of us could have fixed each other's coffees or breakfasts. It was a familiar, comfortable routine. We were a family too. Our conversations were normally about nothing, and we were usually shouting across to the opposite table, sometimes getting yelled at by the waitress for being too loud. "Customers are complaining," she'd say, but they were all blue-collar workers like us, talking the same bullshit.

My last morning with the county I sat back in my seat, next to Pip, who sat back too when he noticed I wasn't talking much.

I knew I wasn't coming back. No one else did. "What's up," he said.

I tried to decide which fragmented thought to grab out of my head and offer. The one that came out was not the one I had intended on giving.

"I'm coming over tonight," I said. "Around seven. Will you be alone?"

"Aren't I usually?" he said. But I knew he'd recently been dating some girl.

When I got there, we downed a couple shots of Jack and drank our beers. Although I'd never been to his place before, I didn't bother looking around. I didn't want it to become familiar or comfortable like the diner. I'd miss the diner, I didn't want to miss his place.

"You're quiet," he said.

I shrugged.

"Something on your mind?"

I poured two double shots for both of us.

"I haven't had sex in a very long time. Are you interested?"

He didn't answer. He sat forward and put his shot glass down. I think he was going to say no, but I was too aggressive for a no. I put my hand over the zipper of his pants, giving him something to think about before he answered.

"Okay," he said quietly, but it wasn't an okay let's do it, rather an okay, what's going on here. But as far as I was concerned, he'd said, Okay, so I sat up and pulled my shirt off.

At four a.m. I went into the family room for my clothes. He didn't follow so I went back to the bedroom where he lay with a drugged, happy look. I was tired and ready to leave, ready to pick up my new rig, call Buzz and tell him I was going back on the road again. To tell Agnes, I didn't know what.

"I don't think I've ever experienced anything quite like that," he said with a euphoric smile.

I nodded.

"Have dinner with me tonight."

"I'm leaving," I told him.

"Or Saturday night. We can keep the dating quiet. I know you like privacy."

"Dating?" I asked him. "I thought we were just having sex."

"It was nothing more than that?"

I sighed. I was no good at this stuff. I said, "You know why I like eating at the diner better than at home?"

"Because at the diner you have company?"

I shook my head no. "Because at the diner I can get up and leave without having to clean up the mess."

"You want this to be a diner meal?" he asked, hurt. Jesus, crushed. Weren't there any men out there anymore who just wanted to mess around?

Though it made me feel like a shit, I said, "Yeah, I just want this to be a diner meal." Then I did what my father always did when he and my mother disagreed, I got up and left.

Sometimes I thought about dinner growing up at my family's house. My mother and I spent most weekdays eating alone. During my teenage years we ran out of things to say. She wasn't interested in knowing that an engine has a special lubrication system that gets oil to its components—like the piston and valves—so they work. She'd stare through me when I talked about anything mechanical. It was almost like she could make herself disappear before my very eyes. Her eyes would center in on an invisible point, and like a black hole, the rest of her would get sucked in after them.

When she asked frivolous questions about cheerleading try-outs or school dances, all things I wasn't engaged in, I made up answers because it was easier that way. When my father came home from a run, we were both let off the hook, and I assume she was as relieved as I was. But his leaving again was unavoidable.

After our first meal together, my mother would say the exact same thing as if she didn't already know what the answer would be. "You'll be home early this week, won't you, Daniel?"

She'd stopped calling him Danny after I was born.

And he'd say, I have a load that needs to go to—anywhere, everywhere, and usually somewhere far from Central New York, like Seattle, or Houston, or Denver. In all likelihood, he wouldn't be home for another week, but he never said that. Instead, he'd say, "I'll be back as soon as I can, Ann, you know that."

My mother would get up and wash dishes to give herself time to grieve. She never made a sound, but when I'd bring my plate to her, her eyelashes would be clumpy, her eyes humid; they'd have that far away vapory look. I always had a feeling she was thinking about what life would have been like if she had married someone other than my father. When I was older, I realized her eyes were like crystal balls that had shown me a glimpse of my future.

When I was little, I remember listening to my mother cry at night, when my father was gone for weeks at a time. After more of her tears than I could stand to let fall, I'd go to her, climb into the bed and let her hold me against her, her bitter words as hot on my head as her tears. "I love him," she'd say, "but don't ever make the mistake of marrying someone who isn't around. The loneliness is enough to make you want to die."

Her words were always with me, especially when I was old enough to understand. As an adult, I was as lonely as I would have been if I had married a trucker myself. In each of my serious relationships I'd wonder if this was truly it. Each man had told me he loved me, had told me that now there was someone to take care of me, I could quit my job, stay home, enjoy life. The instant it happened with each, I felt myself detach, as though I had suddenly traveled hundreds of miles away from myself. In retrospect, I see that I didn't share much with them anyway. I always held back, even when I tried not to.

I remember my first date at sixteen. My mother was certain I'd bring home a dumpy shop-class boy. Instead, I brought home the angelic chorus boy. She actually smiled at him, though it was a smile that bordered on mockery, like the two of us were in on an inside joke. Except I didn't get it. My father clapped him on

the shoulder and the boy winced. It was then I knew I didn't
want a man who was man enough to stand up to my father, but
a man who was woman enough to stand up to my mother.

Because I didn't know or care about matters of love and
marriage, rather than letting the two of them spend quality time
together when he was home, I'd hurry my father out to the
rental garage, where we'd work on an engine or machine that
I'd taken apart to study. She'd sit at the dinner table, drinking
coffee, sewing, still waiting for him to come home to her.

Winter in Central New York is nine months long. By the end,
you just want it to be over yet it isn't uncommon to have a
late snow storm on Mother's Day in May. The last time that
happened people left their houses to study the sky. They stared
quizzically, as if tiny UFOs were falling from outer space. It
wasn't just a few random flakes either, the snow pellets were
coming down so hard, it was as though we were under attack.

Nor is it unusual to have snow in early October. Malls hurry
to put Christmas decorations out, Santas show up skinny. When
snow flies in October, we're sure to have a white Christmas.
When snow flies in October, we're even more sure to have a
rough winter.

Starting around November (earlier if necessary), we partnered up, tuned and washed out our plows, and then headed
for the roads. The plows were our home away from home;
we decorated them accordingly. My last three years on the
job, Buzz and I were partners. We painted the front quarter
panels on our plow black, with a red flame across the middle.
Buzz had pictures of his wife and children taped all around
the cab. It was like living inside a scrap book. I thought about
putting up pictures of my parents and Bobby, but didn't want
the reminders, especially of Bobby. His picture reminded me of
what he believed in: you had to be true to the things you loved,
that you had to fight for them no matter what it cost. For him
it was family and trucking. Before he died, he almost had me
convinced of the same, but I gave up on both when I lost him.

Deena and the kids had to be enough for both Buzz and me.

One of Buzz's sons made us a nifty ceramic ashtray, blue with white speckles. He even made indentations where we could safely place up to four cigarettes. Over the course of the years it was dropped, banged, chipped, and chewed upon by Barley, who rode with us throughout the winter. But no matter how bad a state it was in, it was never replaced by any other ashtray.

Deena bought each of us wool blankets and travel pillows that we kept behind one of the seats. Behind the other was a red and white cooler for our drinks and food. The cooler, like the ashtray, had seen better days. It had more holes than a pockmarked teenager. Even with all these little household things, there was still room for Barley and his essentials. We were never able to control his gas issues or the snot and saliva that shot out of his nose when he sneezed so we suffered through them because we loved him.

My first year on the job, I was partnered up with Dennis. It was no accident. I was purposely put with him because the men didn't want a woman working the roads. I should have been sitting behind a desk in a pretty skirt and a top that revealed just the right amount of cleavage. I was punished before being given a chance, and making Dennis work with a woman was an insult to him because he wasn't liked. They figured one of us would quit. I was tempted to all right, but then toward the end of the winter something happened, and everything changed.

This was my first winter on the job yet even new, I was sick and tired of Dennis's bullshit, his coming on to me, his sexist remarks, his disgusting jokes and sexually explicit conduct. There seemed to be no limit to his pubescent behavior. He'd read his porn magazines and rub himself outside his pants. But the last straw came when he licked his tongue up and down at a woman while we sat at a red light. I sat up and yelled, "You're a filthy pig. It's no wonder no one wants anything to do with you. This time, I'm bringing you in to the foreman."

"Go ahead," he said. "They're looking for a reason to get rid of you, anyway."

He was right. I knew they'd say there'd never been a complaint of this sort before. Men were men and if I couldn't handle it, I should look for employment with the county in another department. Dennis had me, he knew I'd keep my mouth shut, so he continued his escapades, like hanging condoms from my locker, cutting the lock off it every week, hiding my hard hat, or siphoning the gas out of our truck so it looked like I didn't gas up.

I am, by nature, a very patient woman.

Then at the beginning of spring the opportunity came.

The crew was having breakfast at the diner, when a pretty woman walked in. Dennis said, "A pussy like that deserves a man like me."

"You wouldn't know what to do with one if it fell on your face," I said.

That simple line carried so much weight. Because of it I emerged from the game a winner. I was clapped on the back, sheathed with a robe of gold, lavished with praise and applause. Soon they would usher me to the invisible throne where only those who could produce spectacular insults were allowed to sit. Thankfully, that next winter, Buzz pulled rank, and he and I became plowing partners.

Working with your partner all winter long, you can develop a tight bond that not a single person in the world can break. It was like that for Buzz and me. Being out on the roads in bad weather is like being on a battlefield. You never abandon your partner, no matter what. You call in sick only if you're on death's bed. You come to know your partner better than a child knows his father, a wife knows her husband. At times, I wondered if Deena was jealous of me, of all those hours Buzz and I spent together.

My mother had been jealous of my father's world. She hated his trucker friends, men who would come to us for a home-cooked meal, a hot shower, a clean bed. They would come even when my father was out on runs, and my mother would lock herself in her room until they left. When I got older, I was the one who cooked for them. I listened to their stories. I begged them to paint pictures of places I longed to see: the Alamo, Little Bighorn, Death Valley, Mount Rushmore.

I didn't want to be stuck; I didn't want to be lonely, miserable; I didn't want to be my mother.

But here's what I didn't understand. All that yearning to be out on the road, just like he was, would lead me to the one place I didn't want to be. Sitting in a diner alone, walking out alone, and leaving the mess for someone else to pick up.

Salmacis

The element of water Gives and receives strange forms...And there
are other streams...whose waters affect the mind as well as body...
You have heard of Salmacis...where a swallow of the water Will
drive you raving mad or hold You rigid In catatonic lethargy.

—Ovid

As usual, I'm off.

Before I left, Jesse asked me if I'd be coming back sooner
or later.

"Sooner," I told him, leaving out that New York used to be
my home base, but not anymore. Without invitation or good
reason, it's become the Yellow Submarine, where Jesse Reid
lives.

He said, "Instead of packing everything up, why don't you
leave your things in your room?" After three months, that's
exactly what it's become.

"I don't want to take up space," I said, leaving the sentence
open-ended.

"We don't use these rooms anyway. You're the first since
Gary had a cousin in from Arkansas a year ago."

"Then why'd you let me?" I asked.

Pulling out a cigarette gave Jesse time to think. Pulling out
two doubled the time, which is what he did.

"Don't take this the wrong way, but you looked a little lost.
Like you needed a dose of some fine, home-grown southern
tending to. Like a sheep." Jesse smirked.

"So that would make you Little Bo Peep?"

Jesse laughed. "Now don't get me wrong, I ain't taken you to
raise—" His voice trailed off into more laughter.

"Of course not. You wouldn't want your southern friends to
know you were taking care of a Yankee."

Smiling, I put all but a small travel bag back in the room.

"You going to unpack?"

Jesse doesn't like disorder, so I unpacked while he watched.

"You'll be gone long?"

"I'll aim for a couple weeks, maybe less."

"Maybe more."

I nodded, because I never really knew.

"Easter will be here 'fore you know it," Jesse said.

"Few weeks," I added. "Do you go home or something?"

Jesse laughed harshly. "I haven't been back to Alabama since I left at thirteen."

"So, what do you do about holidays?"

"What did you do this past Christmas?" Jesse tossed back.

He didn't know numbers, but he knew that truckers never stop. We work over three hundred days a year and haul more than six-hundred billion-ton-miles of long-distance freight.

"I spent Christmas on the road."

"For die hards like *you* we host holiday parties."

"So, if I'm back for Easter—" I hoped he'd finish my sentence for me.

"I'll have a nice Easter basket filled with chocolates waitin' for you. But I'll expect to see you in an Easter bonnet."

"And an egg hunt?"

Jesse's smile widened. "The biggest you ever did see. It might be entertaining to watch burly truckers searching for Easter eggs. I'll have to fill 'em with cigarettes."

We laughed, bowed our heads. It was all so juvenile.

Then I said, "I guess I should get a move on." I pulled my wallet out of my back pocket. "Should I pay Gary now?"

"Put that up. You're not paying for the room. We'll take it out in trade." Another smirk.

Oh yes, I thought, yes, we will.

We walked out of the bar and across the gravel parking lot to where Old Snort was. Jesse eyed her curiously, like a child.

"Can I look inside?"

"Help yourself."

He climbed in through the passenger door and I got in my seat.

"This is something," he said looking at the dash and at the sleeper. Then he took hold of my hand. "You'll drive carefully." It was a question and statement rolled into one. "We'll be waitin' for you." He got out and slammed the door, then came around to the driver's side. "You might need this," he said, and held his silver lighter up. I leaned out the window and took it. I felt like he'd just given me his high school ring.

I couldn't help myself. I said, "Does this mean we're going steady?"

He shrugged, then laughed uncomfortably. His cheeks reddened.

"I'll be here," was how he answered. That was enough. "You take care."

"Don't worry. Me and Old Snort know the routine."

I'm on a long-distance haul that's taking me through Michigan. Most long-distance drivers prefer driving at night when the smokies are on skeleton graveyard shifts and the four wheelers are off the road. It's like living in the world alone, like knowing what the crash of trees sounds like when no one else is around. This kind of drive puts you face-to-face with the granddaddy of loneliness. If you can get through without cracking, you can make it through anything.

I've had my fair share of making it through things. Dodging animals, deer mostly, a couple fox, and, once, a coyote. Several years ago, a group of us in a convoy were moving through Virginia, and running alongside us were eight deer, inching their way closer to the highway. It would have been a beautiful sight if I hadn't known one of them was going to die. Our Front Door moved into the hammer lane, and most of us in the Rocking Chair, or middle, followed without getting four wheelers between us. I watched in my side mirror as one deer ran itself into the bumper of the driver behind me. It was pure suicide. Even at our speed and distance, I saw its blood splatter, its neck break. Like the military, we're trained to look for enemy assaults. We should be followed, not passed. It landed on an impatient four wheeler trying to pass us in the granny lane. It was messy, and certainly slowed our driver down, but it wasn't as disabling to him as it was to the four wheeler. If we hit a deer just right, we won't necessarily immobilize ourselves. Moose, on the other hand, can destroy a diesel. One trucker who survived it said it was like running into the side of a mountain. Imagine, he'd said, what it would do to a four wheeler.

I've hit deer, skunks, moles, squirrels, chipmunks, and possums. I've hit dogs and cats. Turtles and snakes. I've even hit chickens, birds, ducks, guard rails, and big pieces of tire that we call alligators (because they look like them), sunning themselves across the road.

Making it through goes beyond hit and runs, though. It always comes back to the elements. The worst I've ever experienced was a sandstorm in Arizona. Every vehicle on the road pulled over and turned off the engines because the air vents were sucking in rocks and sand. I thought for certain the front windshield would bust through. Tornadoes are bad, but not as bad as sandstorms. At least you can see the twister. In the upper Michigan-Ohio region the sky turns green before a tornado hits. That's when you start driving like hell.

Snow is bad, too, some worse than others. Heading through Syracuse, New York, to Buffalo one winter (normally a two-and-a-half-hour drive), I got on the thruway and there was no worker in the toll booth. It took me nearly six hours to get into Buffalo, pushing snow with my front bumper the whole way. When I did arrive, the man in the toll booth looked at me astounded. He said, "You got a ticket?"

"Naw, couldn't find anyone."

"It's no wonder. The damn thruway's been closed for nearly seven hours."

I stuck a hundred toward him, but he said, "Shit, it's a miracle you made it. Keep it."

And now, in Michigan, it's still a vicious winter. My mind,

which should be on the road, focuses on imagining Jesse, naked, in bed with me. I go through a few possible sex scenarios,
well, maybe more, but I also think about more than sex. I think
about Easter with him. I think about possible birthday presents
when May rolls around. Halloween, Thanksgiving, Christmas,
Fourth of July. I think about waking up and making breakfast
together, about driving to the ocean on the motorcycles, about
holding hands, the fireworks exploding in the sky not making
nearly as much racket as those detonating from my heart.

My body is trying to pilot the truck, without my brain,
through the center of a snow band, when a four wheeler slips
out in front of me to pass a pickup. The conditions are nearly
whiteout. Though not yet covered, the roads are still too slick
for such quick movement, and I'm coming up steadily. Here's
something my father taught me: if you can see a truck's tires'
spray, the road hasn't frozen over. If you can't, it's covered with
black ice. If the four wheeler were paying attention, he would
have noticed there was no spray. Here's something Bobby taught
me: four wheelers think truckers can stop on a dime. We can't.

I'm speculating but my guess is that the four wheeler panics
when he sees me moving up fast, so he veers back into the
granny lane without looking. He hits ice and smashes into the
back end of the pickmeup, spinning it counterclockwise and
perpendicular into the hammer line, right in my line of fire.
The passenger in the pickmeup looks up at my headlights and
then right at me, as I aim at her door. For an instant, we make
eye contact. If I swerve, I'll jackknife into the center ditch. If I
continue forward, I'll smash the front passenger side and pitch
the whole truck under my tires. It's a no-win situation.

All this processes through my brain in an instant, and I
don't have time to get nervous, but I do find myself trying to
decide between crashing and possibly never seeing Jesse again
or killing these people. I take my foot off the brake, and as I
begin to swerve left out of the hammer lane onto the shoulder,
I prepare myself for a rough landing. It's probable that I'll tip,
that I'll be killed, and that I'll maybe even take the pickup with

me, but it still seems to be the lesser of two evils. Then the pickup inexplicably shoots backward, clearing the lane. My back end begins fish tailing, and I hope like hell the four wheeler that started this mess is already out of the way. The trailer is beginning to overcome the cab. The only way I can get control now is to stand on the throttle, even over the ice. It's a race for the cab to outrun the back end. It takes a lot of time and a lot of speed over the ice, but it works. It's at this point that my legs start to shake. I want to stop to see if anyone is injured, but by the time I have control, I'm too far ahead to help. Though it goes against my moral obligation, I keep moving and radio in.

I've had many close calls over the years, and I've always gotten out to assess the damage and help. It makes me think about my parents and the trucker who killed them, and how he tried to keep going except that two of his tires blew and a piece of my father's truck was sticking out of his truck's grill like a bayonet. There were two eyewitnesses, and both felt the need to give me the blow-by-blow details. How my father tried to swerve out of the way. How the trucker barreled into the vehicle with such force the windows of their pickup shot out. How the roof was smashed down to the floor, which I'm sure was the reason why the medical examiner could only go by dental records. It was information I didn't need to know.

Truckers like that guy shame the rest of us; he's why I left the business the first time. At night, in my dreams, I'd be sitting in my truck, and my mother would be in the passenger seat staring at me. She never spoke but her eyes would say, *You've chosen them over us.* That's why I stopped driving. I had already disappointed her enough, and so had my father. I suspect that's why he'd stopped driving by then too. Instead, he picked up a job at a garage, maybe thinking he'd try to patch up a marriage that had been taken for granted. When I came home from runs, dinner would be hot on the table, and my father would ask me questions about things I was engaged in, like what kind of freight I'd hauled, and the places I'd seen. We had a common language, and my mother, well, she just sat there and listened, or pretended to, and waited until it was her turn.

She'd say, "You'll be home early this week, won't you, Danny?"

And I could have said, I have a load that needs to go to—anywhere, everywhere, usually somewhere far like Seattle, or Houston, or Denver. In all likelihood, I wouldn't be home for another week or two, but I never said that. I'd say, "I'll be back as soon as I can, Mom, you know that."

The one thing my mother never lost as she grew older, was her reflective look. What if she'd gone to college instead of getting married, what if she'd stayed single, what if she'd married someone else? I'd want to say to her, *But then I wouldn't be Danny, I'd be someone else.* I wouldn't say it because I was afraid she'd say, *Exactly.* So instead, I hugged her. She was shorter than me, stout, a woman who really filled your arms when you hugged her. I could see why my father loved her.

"Just be happy for me, Mom," I'd say, before looking into her eyes. If only I had realized they were like crystal balls, showing me a glimpse of my future.

Then my father would hug the both of us, then ask me, "You want to go over to the garage?"

And I'd say, "I've got plans tonight, Dad."

By then I understood the matters of love and marriage, even though I'd never experienced either. But I knew that the two of them needed to spend quality time together. As left out as I felt, I knew it wasn't about me anymore.

When I'd get home at night, they'd be sitting at the dinner table, drinking coffee. She'd usually be sewing, while he'd be fiddling with a small machine, a VCR or cassette player, for extra cash, like that's what they did every single night of the week. All along, they'd been waiting and waiting for me to come home to them, perhaps thinking that one day something terrible would happen and I would never walk through the door again.

The one thing time offers is experience. There's a first for everything, just like there's a last. One of those nights would be the last, except not for me, but for them.

Seventeen days after I left the Yellow Submarine, I walk through the door with my duffle bag draped over my shoulder, like a soldier who'd been away at war. After that near crash, I feel like one.

As soon as he sees me, Gary retrieves a bottle of beer from a secret stash and places it in front of the stool next to Jesse's. Gary watches as Jesse walks over to me. His eyes narrow as Jesse greets me with a half a hug, then he shrugs, as if he doesn't know what to make of it, and goes off to the dart board.

It's how I've felt since Jesse gave me his lighter. I'm not sure what to make of it, either. I wonder if even Jesse knows what he's feeling. One minute he's flirting, the next he's reserved. But I can't complain or worry about that now. Now he's got his arm around me. Now he's leading me to my appointed stool. Now he's taking my bag from me, walking over to the kitchen window, putting in a dinner order, and then disappearing to put my bag away.

He's happy to see me, and I feel everything inside me lift and spin. Sunshine shoots out my fingertips and eyes and toes. I feel almost holy. And then my supper is placed in front of me. It's the exact same meal that was put in front of me my first night here. Jesse is sitting on his stool next to me, talking to a trucker. The place is packed, the music loud, the smoke rising from the ground as if we're in a swamp.

Jesse sees me staring down at my plate and says, "Is everything all right, darlin'?"

"I don't want to be rude, but I really don't think I can eat this."

"Why? What's wrong with it?" He takes my fork and pokes at it as if he's making sure it's dead.

"I'm sorry, Jesse, but I cannot eat a breaded hog jowl. The thought gags me."

As I say it, Jesse is taking a big gulp of beer. He puts the glass on the bar top and throws his hand over his mouth so he doesn't spit it out. Then he's off his stool, walking with his hand still covering his mouth, his body bent. He moves to the kitchen window and plants himself, leaning against the wall until he swallows. Then he lets out the laugh that's been trapped in his mouth.

"You asshole!" I yell and that makes him laugh harder, louder.

"That's a breaded chicken breast," he manages to say, and starts laughing all over.

"You told me it was a hog jowl," I yell, and his body bounces into a whole new fit of laughter. "I'll get you back," I say threatening him, even though I'm laughing too.

Just as I slice my cutlet, Gary stands on a stool and begins ringing the bell hanging from the ceiling. Customers rush up to get a drink before the singing of "Yellow Submarine." Jesse goes behind the bar to help serve. Earle comes out of the kitchen to pass out the guitar and the bells. This will be my second time, so it still feels new, exciting, refreshing. With only fifteen minutes to do so, Jesse and Gary pour close to a hundred beers.

By the time the song begins, Jesse hands me a bottle, reaches for a harmonica from under the bar, and puts his arm around my shoulders. He's moved us to the center of the bar so that I can ring the ocean-buoy bell during the instrumentals. It's an honor. People who've never met have their arms around each others' shoulders. Most of them don't belong to the upper class, they never have and never will. Most of them live in double-wides, or small apartments like I did as a child and adult, most of them will never own a new car or even a decent used one. Most of them will never own designer clothes or costly jewelry. Most of them belong to the same class of people I do. But here, we're important, we belong. Jesse and Gary make sure of it.

We're singing as loud as we can. Jesse only knows how to play parts of certain Beatles' songs on his harmonica, but he does it skillfully. As we sing, I watch him closely. For a man whose being seems always heavy with disappointment, who has a tendency toward depression, his demeanor is relieved, his smile genuinely festive. His eyes are lighthearted, and really rather lively. I know that in these moments, as short lived as they are, Jesse is happy; as we sing, I realize it's become a goal of mine to produce these moments more often.

After the singing, we talk until the bar closes at 3:30. Jesse tells Gary that the two of us will clean up. As we clean, we smoke and drink and laugh once in a while, but mostly chat. We scrub tables, chairs, and stools, haul the garbage to the dumpster out back, sit at a picnic table, and smoke some more.

It's here, at this time and this place, on a cool, clear night with the stars shining, that I tell Jesse about the way my parents died. And then, because in a sense one is connected to the other, I have to tell him about the things I see.

"Do you think I'm crazy?" I ask.

"Of course not. I think the mind can cause us to see certain things and act certain ways."

It's a vague statement and I have the feeling there's more to it, but Jesse isn't inclined to give details.

"I wonder if I drove by where it happened if I'd see it. How could I deal with seeing my parents subjected to that all over again? It would be cruel to do that to them, wouldn't it?"

"It's probably not a good idea. For you, anyway."

He sits back and rests his elbows on the table. His leather jacket opens, and I have to stop myself from reaching in and wrapping my arms around his waist.

"What do you mean by that?"

Jesse sticks his fingers in his shirt pocket and pulls out the pack of cigarettes.

"What I mean," he says, the cigarette bouncing between his lips. He stops talking and lights it. He holds one up to me, but I shake my head no. He removes a piece of tobacco from his tongue. He says, "I'd pay good money to see my daddy—well, I don't want to discriminate, so I'll say my mama too—in that kind of pain. Nice long torture." His eyes glaze as he stares into space. "Nice and long and slow; very slow. You know, like cutting off one piece of them at a time. Carving them like turkeys.

Fingers and then toes and then…well, other parts, too. Yes, I reckon I'd give up one of my bikes to see that."

I put my hand on his thigh and he looks at me. We have a tendency not to ask each other questions, we just let each other say what we deem necessary. I've never before let anyone know I'm listening, and hope he knows, by the touch of my hand, that I really am.

"But you," he says, scooching a little closer to me, then putting his arm behind my shoulders so that it rests on the table… just in case I misunderstand. "From what I've gathered, your daddy meant a great deal to you, and your mama too. But I think your daddy meant more."

I give a half nod. "My father'd be gone for weeks at a time. Well, as long as I was gone this last time, but as a kid it seemed like forever. I know it was hard for my mother but sometimes, Jesse, I think it was harder for me. Doesn't it seem weird that I was closer to him than my mother? Do you think that's why I turned out like this?"

"Like what, darlin'?"

"Not very pretty. Not very feminine."

"Is gender really important to you?"

I shrug, unsure, and ask, "In terms of what?"

"You seem to think you're more masculine than feminine. Which I don't think is true, by the way. Have you ever been asked out by a woman?"

I laugh uncomfortably. "Not that I'm aware of."

"If you were, would you think there's something wrong with you?"

"I don't know," I say, and think for a moment. "No, I guess not."

"If I were gay, would you like me less?"

No! No! No! my head screams. *Anything but that.* Disappointment churns my stomach.

"Of course not, Jesse."

He nods.

"I like you the way you are," Jesse says hesitantly, as though

I might think his opinion is irrelevant. "And, for the record, I think you're very pretty."

"You do?"

"I do."

His arm seems to tighten around my shoulders, but it's just as possible I'm imagining it. Near or far, it's there, and, though I feel safer than I ever have, my insecurities eat away at me, and I make myself believe that I need some verbal reassurance from him.

"Shouldn't you be throwing in some Whitman quote to make me feel better?" I ask with a smile.

"For you, sugar, anything. 'I am the poet of the Body and I am the poet of the Soul, The pleasures of heaven are with me and the pains of hell are with me, The first I graft and increase upon myself, the latter I translate into a new tongue. I am the poet of the woman the same as the man, And I say it is as great to be a woman as to be a man...' Does that make you feel better?"

No, I think. All it does is nudge the uncertainties I've felt about his sexuality.

When we've finished picking up the bar, we walk slowly to our rooms. In the past, Jesse has stood in the middle of the hall to say good night. This morning is different. I lean against the frame and he stands in front of me. It's hard, in situations like these, not to get my hopes up, even after what he's led me to believe.

He runs his knuckles down the side of my face, and I try not to act like a girl, but it's kind of second nature. He's caught me off guard, and I look down, blush, then chance glancing at him again. Jesse is a man of few words so I know what happens next will be based on body movements, not language. He runs his fingers down one of my cheeks, and then the other. We're close, but he doesn't let the space between our bodies become less. He's down to one finger now, tracing my eyebrows and the bridge of my nose, then my cheek bone. His lips hold a subdued curve: not a smile, not a frown, but a contentment, a pensive bend. Even the lines around his eyes have softened.

I am a woman of too many words, and I have to speak. I'm thinking how there are only a few patches on his face where there are whiskers. Maybe twenty on the bottom of his chin, some around his sideburns and under his nose, and some on the very bottom of his jawbone.

I stupidly say it. "Your cheeks are so smooth." My words are like BB's out of a gun. Not deadly but damaging enough.

His eyebrows push together and he frowns. "Good night, Danny. I'm glad you've returned safely."

I go into my room, walk over to the wall, and bang my head against it.

Then I move to the mirror and say through clenched teeth, "You are a fucking moron."

I'm usually up early, but after last night, I don't wake up until nearly one. When I finally make my way to the bar, Gary pours me a cup of coffee and I plant myself on my stool.

"Long night?" he asks.

I nod. "Where's Jesse?"

"Gone. He's been gone since eight this morning."

A customer leaves and Gary goes over, wipes the bar, then comes back to me.

"Did he say where he was off to?"

Gary shakes his head. "There are times when you don't ask Jesse questions. This morning was one of them."

"Did he take one of his scoots?"

"Ma'am?"

"One of his Harleys?"

"He took the Duo-Glide. He always takes the Duo-Glide when he needs to think."

I groan and drop my head on my forearms. Gary pours more coffee.

"I need advice, Gary. Is it me? Should I back off? Whenever I think it's going nowhere, Jesse does something, gives me some sign. And then the next thing I know, he's as cold as ice."

"He's a complicated man, Danny. And very private. He has many acquaintances. Lots of them are friends, but none he'd confide in."

"But you're not one of those people."

Gary smiles. "It took him years to open up to me."

I notice a pack of Jesse's cigarettes on top of his tablet, so I lean over and grab it. As I do, the paperweight next to it catches my eye. "What the hell is this?" I ask him.

Gary peers at it. "It's a thing that holds paper down."

I cluck my tongue against the roof of my mouth. "Not the paperweight, the bug."

"Ain't you ever seen a snail?"

"Why in hell would anyone put a snail inside a paperweight?"

"The snail happens to be Jesse's favorite mollusk. He had that 'specially made. And it wasn't cheap, neither."

I give him an annoyed look. "People don't have favorite insects. Insects function as irritants and food. Until they're eaten or die, they spend their lives pestering humans."

"Uh-uh, you're not listening, I said they're mollusks not insects. You asked for advice, and I'm going to give you some: don't say what you just said to Jesse." I can't tell if he's kidding or not. "They happen to be intriguing little things, in case you're interested."

It's easier to give in. "Okay, enlighten me."

Gary leans down. "The snail is the only creature that carries its house on its back."

"What about the turtle?"

"Don't bother me with particulars. A snail has only one foot and it leaves a slimy trail as it moves. The trail keeps the foot from getting scratched. A snail also has a tongue that's covered with teeth, and it has its eyes at the end of long stalks. When it gets real scared, it pulls the whole stalk into its head. But the most amazing thing about snails is, they're hermaphrodites. That means it's both male and female. Now there's some interesting facts about snails."

He's left me speechless. I'm not sure I want to or am even capable of engaging in this conversation.

"Do you want to know how they mate?" Gary asks.

I hold my hand up to stop him. "I'm okay with what you've given me."

"Listen to me, Danny, because this is important. Just because snails can adapt to their surroundings doesn't mean they live easily. Snails are independent, but they need to be loved. Don't discriminate against the snail," he warns.

I can't help but think the conversation has gone beyond me, so I just agree that I won't discriminate. I'm about to tell him that I'll kill all insects equally, but who knows how he'll take it. Instead, I find myself getting sentimental again. "It's just that I've never met anyone like him."

"That's because Jesse's special, Danny."

"I know, Gary. Believe me, I know. Give me something to work with, please."

"Why? Why should he trust you after just a few months? Why should I?"

I have a weak case. I'll look foolish showing off the lighter Jesse gave me. It's a lighter. But then I think, well, it's his lighter, so I pull it out and hold it to my mouth and nose, and then present it to Gary as though it were a diamond ring.

At first, Gary shakes his head. He says, "He's more than a friend to me, he's a brother. He took me in when I needed a place to go."

"What do you think I'm going to do to him?"

Exhaling, Gary shrugs. "You've already made an impact on him. Nights when you're on the road, and he hears a truck pull in, he waits to see if it's you comin' through that door." He shrugs again.

"Last night he told me a little about his parents."

Gary looks at me with surprise.

"Please, Gary. Help me just a little."

He finally nods and tells me this story that Jesse told him long ago.

...It's a Saturday afternoon, one o'clock, June, hot in Alabama, and Jesse is eleven. He's been forced to watch his father and three brothers rape a girl. To his father, this is Jesse's initiation into manhood; the earlier the better. When the brothers are taking their turns, the father gives a detailed and proud commentary of their abilities, their technique, their command. Before the father can make his fourth boy have a turn, Jesse has run home hoping his mother will, for once, provide safety. The mother is in a small, dark room, a room that has been adorned in religion. She's weaving as if drunk. She's speaking in tongues, nearly frothing at the mouth, chanting so fast, so incomprehensibly, she's worked herself into a convulsion.

Enraged, the father has followed. The child is trapped between them; they are his bookends of the two things that scare and confuse him most: Sex and Religion. The father slaps the mother out of her meditation. Blood spreads through the creases in her bottom lip.

"Do something with the boy," he says to her.

She has a difficult time getting herself together. Her dress is twisted, her mouth bleeding, and she's been gripping a crown of thorns that have punctured her hands. The delay has given the father enough time to crush the boy's head under his arm, and whisper, "I ain't raising a pussy faggot." Then he screams at the mother, "You done made him like this."

The mother is afraid to get near Jesse. She's repulsed, ashamed. She won't move toward either one of them.

"Make him into a man," the father threatens. "Or I'll kill the both of you." He pushes Jesse at the mother, but she doesn't catch him, she lets him fall.

"Purge yourself of ills," she says to Jesse and goes back to swaying. "Wage your spiritual warfare against evil."

The father takes Jesse by the hair and pushes him into a small closet. It's filled with crowns, bibles, crosses. Jesse tries to throw his slim frame against the door to keep it from closing but he's too small, too slight. He tears at the door with his fingernails, then kicks out with his foot in search of critters.

He's deathly afraid of snakes and the dark. When he's confident there's nothing living at the bottom of the closet, he kneels to look through the keyhole, and tries to keep himself from whimpering too loudly. The mother has begun to pray. The words start out slow, comprehensible.

"Repent," she hisses. "Power comes with the holy ghost. The holy ghost moves up on me."

The father has no tolerance for it. He's so incensed by her religion that he pushes her to her hands and knees and enters her forcefully. The louder and faster she prays, the harder and faster he shoves himself into her.

"Let it shine Jesus, repent, repent, come see the lord come and get it. Thank you, Jesus."

It's as though he's pushing the prayers out of her. It's become a contest. Louder...harder. Jesse curls into a ball and covers sensitive ears with sensitive hands. In a few hours he'll try, for the first time, to kill himself.

After his story, Gary gives me my first beer of the day. After his story, I need it. Nice, long, slow torture. Now, what Jesse said makes sense. "Didn't he ever tell anyone?"

"He was a child," Gary says in Jesse's defense. "Besides, who do you think would've cared?"

"But what they did to him, what they did to that girl," I argue. "They should've been held accountable."

"He was as much a victim as the girl was."

And he was just a boy, I tell myself. Just a vulnerable boy.

"How many times has he tried?" I whisper, feeling sick and troubled.

"A handful. He got a little more daring each time."

Is this why he can't get close to me, because he sees me as a sexual predator like his father and brothers? Or does he see it in himself? Would there be more attempts now, now that I've interfered in his life? Did he try again today?

"What should I do?" I ask, and get ready to do whatever Gary tells me to. Search for him, pack my bags and leave, anything.

"Stay put."

I do, all day and all night. With each passing hour, with each beer and shot I gulp down, the possibilities become grimmer. I'm certain he's gone to the shore and thrown himself into the ocean. Or maybe he's driven his bike off a cliff, or into a bridge abutment. All because I've indicated that I want to sleep with him, that I want him to do the one thing he's most afraid of. I make Earle come out and drink with me so I'll stop thinking about it. But, by nine, the kitchen is too busy for him to leave. I direct my panic at Gary.

"He's fine," Gary assures me. He doesn't seem the least bit worried. "He called an hour ago. Here." He puts another shot in front of me and goes down the bar to wait on a group of customers. The bar is as jammed as I am drunk. As he pours a beer, Gary tucks the portable phone between his ear and shoulder, and calls Carl, another bartender.

"I can't keep up," I hear him holler into the receiver, and I let my worry disappear just like that. He stands in front of me and pours four beers.

"Must be a full moon," he jokes, and takes money from over my shoulder.

"I hope Jesse isn't on your payroll. Man, I'd fire his ass for taking off like that."

Gary actually stops pouring beers and looks at me. I light him a cigarette, so he'll take a break.

"Jesse hired me to do this job so he wouldn't have to worry about time."

"What do you mean, Jesse hired you? He told me that he helps you when you need it."

Gary has stopped working all together. He's just standing there staring at me like I'm the world's biggest idiot.

"Danny, you do realize that Jesse owns the bar, don't you? I work for him, Carl works for him, Earle works for him. How in the name of Jesus do you think he's able to buy them Harleys?"

For the second time today I feel shocked, but this time oddly stirred. Gary walks down the bar to wait on another customer then comes back again.

"I've made up my mind, I'm going to make a move," I tell him as he pours a shot of Jack and hands it to me.

"This is from that fella down there," Gary says, and points to a trucker. I lift my shot at him. "So, what exactly are you gonna do?"

"I don't know, it depends on the situation. Like if you told me this was from Jesse, that would be a whole 'nother story."

"Ma'am?"

"I'd take him to my room and give him a proper thank you."

"Really?"

"Oh yeah," I say, talking it up. And I suspect Gary knows I'm talking out of my head because I'm drunk and feeling cocky, so he puts me to the challenge.

"Well good, 'cause here's your chance."

He eyes me as Jesse stands on the stool to ring the 10:15 warning bell.

I feel too drunk to sing, plus Jesse hasn't exactly approached me, so a dash of gloom makes me not only drunk but a little mean. Even Jesse doesn't seem to be into it as much as he usually is. But no one is paying attention to our bad moods. The bar has a mood of its own, and it's cheery and snug.

With the new knowledge that Jesse owns the bar, I study the Beatles collectibles more closely, an original *Yesterday and Today* album worth a small fortune, the signed posters and photographs. Drumsticks. Concert tickets. T-shirts. And more. All owned by Jesse. All of it, every last thing in this bar, including me, if he wants me, owned by Jesse.

"You're looking a little too serious for someone who's run up a three-digit bar tab," he says.

And he's right. The alcohol has put everything into perspective for me. I know what I have to do. I pull a credit card out of my wallet.

"I'm just foolin'," he says, though his face doesn't reflect it.

"It's making sense now," I tell him.

Gary won't accept my credit card, so I take all the cash in my wallet and throw it over the bar. Most of it lands on the floor, but I don't care. I turn around and walk away.

There isn't a whole lot to pack. I've never been much of a collector. Collecting things means feeling safe, and security like that means settling down. And settling down means love and marriage and things I never thought I wanted in my life. It doesn't matter anyway, not to Jesse.

"Danny, what's gotten into you?" Jesse has followed me to my room.

"I'm leaving."

"You're drunk."

"You've been lying to me and leading me on."

"I told you I couldn't give you what you wanted. I told you that from the very beginning."

"Then why in hell do you treat me the way you do?"

"I don't treat you any differently than I treat—"

"Your other customers?" I spit out.

"That's not what I was going to say."

"It makes sense now. I know what's going on. You're a businessman. You've got money. You're educated. I'm just a low-life trucker."

Jesse doesn't even argue. He just stands there shaking his head.

"No? Then you must be gay, because no man in his right mind walks away knowing he can get laid."

"You're right."

The words stop my tirade and I spin to look at him. As long as he didn't admit it, getting together was at least a slim possibility, but now I know he's off-limits to me.

"You're right. No man in his right mind would turn you away."

Like the snail, he pulls his stalks into his head, crosses the hall, opens his door and, like a snail, slides through without a sound.

It doesn't take long before I go across the hall and knock. When Jesse opens the door, his face holds two contradictory expressions. The first, the one I prefer, passes too quickly. He's glad I'm there. The second is dismal. He looks down at the rug and sighs, a sigh of disappointment that sounds worse than the word No. I have put us in the predicament he's purposely been avoiding. I try to smile, but instead take a step back, disappointed too, disillusioned. I want to ask him why he doesn't want me the way I want him, but it'll sound so pathetic; it's exactly what my ex-lovers would have said. I'd rather suffer and live with the rejection.

"I came to say goodbye."

My words prompt him to look up. His expression has changed again. He's moved by my feelings; I can tell by the way his brows come together. But then, maybe it's sympathy. Jesse reaches his hand out and the back of it grazes my cheek. I want to drop down before him and beg him to have sex with me, but again, it's all about having a tiny bit of self-respect…and something else, something so utterly foreign to me. Something that feels more important than sex.

Jesse takes my fingers in his and leads me into his apartment. He pulls me to him, holding both my hands in his between our bodies, and bends his forehead to mine.

"All I can do is apologize."

"You were right. You told me it wouldn't happen between us. You haven't done anything to apologize for."

That smile again.

"I feel like a perfect fool saying this, but it isn't that I'm not attracted to you. Listen to me, Danny." I've stepped away, afraid that I'm about to become a charity case. But then I'm close to him again and he's saying, "…because I am so very, very attracted to you."

"Then why won't you kiss me?"

"Because if I do, it has to end there, with just a kiss. Is that worth it to you? All these emotions for a kiss? It isn't much of a payoff."

"Yes, Jesse, it is. And besides, maybe you'll want more."

Jesse once called me bold, and it's at this second that I recognize it in myself. Bold got me through a high school program designed for boys. Bold gave me courage to claim the open road, got me a man's job with the county, gave me the resolve to reclaim the world I so haphazardly discarded. Yet, now it seems to work as a repellent. Like two negative sides of a magnet, with every step forward I take, Jesse sidesteps and falls back.

"I want to do all those things people do in the bedroom, but I've learned to live without it. Unlike you, I'm not terribly experienced at this type of thing."

"So, it's because I actively pursue sexual encounters and women aren't supposed to do that."

Now he's insulted me, and I'm ready to leave, but he doesn't loosen his hold.

"You told me once that you were a good listener, but I don't see much proof of that," Jesse tries to tease, but falls short. "The thing is, if you must know, I haven't kissed anyone in a very long time."

"What's a long time? Six months, a year?"

"A little longer. A lot longer."

"I don't care how long it's been. It's like—"

"Riding a bicycle," Jesse interrupts.

"You said it was all about stereotype," I say, trying to argue a point Jesse once made, that though people belong to one or more stereotype families, it's important to strip them down— Shuck 'em like corn, Jesse liked to say—and see what's on the inside.

"That's a cliché," Jesse corrects, and smiles. "Damn, you're stubborn."

"It's one of my better traits," I say, before moving closer again. "I can deal with a..." How to say this delicately? "Sexually transmitted disease. We just need to take precautions."

"That's not it. I've never had a girlfriend, Danny. I've never taken a woman out on a date. I've never taken anyone out on a date. I've never gone to a prom or a movie with anyone. I've never—" He shrugs. "I've never voluntarily gotten into bed and made love to a woman."

So, it isn't like riding a bicycle. It's more like learning to walk.

Jesse closes his eyes for a second and I take advantage of it. Cupping my hand around the back of his neck, I let one finger rub his hair line. That draws out a nice longing sigh. It's better than the other sigh he gave. This one is open ended, there's no finality to it. He doesn't open his eyes so I move my lips in closer.

His brain fails to give him language to express what he's thinking or feeling, though I'm sure if the chapbook of Whitman on the end table could move, it would leap into Jesse's hands and open itself up to a page. He doesn't need to depend on that because his body sends loud enough vibes for me to hear. Is this what it feels like to be stirred to life? A touch that turns your blood into something flammable? His body shivers; we've both been ignited.

He can feel me there, my breath on his chin, my eyes on his mouth, every membrane in my body zeroing in on his lips. It's as nerve-wracking as waiting for a starting gun, the anticipation, the nervousness, the edginess. If he parts his lips even for a breath, I'll take it as a sign to move forward.

We have spent three hours making out. Three glorious, yet exhausting, hours.

We began the same way a toddler learns to walk. Banging and stumbling. At the first go, he failed to turn his head and our noses struck. At the second go, he didn't open his mouth, so I gave gentle instructions. It didn't take long before he was an old hand at it. The finely honed distinguishable subtleties like nibbling and tongue-teasing came in time.

When it comes to sex, Jesse, you've come to the right teacher, I think.

I suggested we lay on the bed, but Jesse kept us in the sitting room. So, we sat on the couch. Twice I placed his hand upon my breast, both times it stiffened with uncertainty.

Just keep it slow, I reminded myself.

Now, I regroup. I decide to familiarize myself with his body the way the pioneers moved across the uncultivated country, slowly and cautiously. Unlike a pioneer, I won't conquer, I'll study the uninhabited region, divide it into parcels and examine until I know what makes the land thrive. I begin with his hand, his palm, his thin wrist, which is covered by a ridiculously large black watchband he must have acquired in the seventies. I pull the leather strap to take it off, but he yanks his arm away and shakes his head.

"We have to begin somewhere," I say.

Jesse hesitates, then reluctantly removes it to reveal two thick white scars. So many stories and secrets are hidden in places we can't see. I lift the wrist and kiss the scars. Jesse tries not to shudder when I do it. I run my tongue along the tracks as though my saliva will heal not just the pinched skin, but the anguish that led him to do it. He covers his mouth with the other hand and waits apprehensively.

I burrow into him like an animal settling in for the winter. He's receptive to it, for the most part, always moving my arms around his waist when I embrace him, but nowhere else. Jesse purrs when I nuzzle him, when my lips skim his neck like a paper-thin rock over water, when my fingertips tickle his skin; he leaves himself unprotected, exposed to the elements. It always comes back to the elements.

Jesse's body is like a lullaby. The rhythm of it rocks me into faith. It opens the door to something I never experienced with other men. I tell him about their needs and expectations. That because it was all so taxing, I couldn't open up to them. We were already drowning in their bullshit; why add mine to it?

"Fear of commitment," he says like an expert, while he's rubbing his hand down my head and neck, so I'll agree to anything he says. "You decided not to fall in love with them before the relationships started."

"I was on the road so much it wouldn't have been fair to any one of them."

"You didn't want to get left behind every week. You didn't want to see yourself staring out the window as an adult, like you did as a child, watching him pull away like your daddy did."

"There was still so much for my dad and me to do, so much to see, so much to talk about," I say. "We always think there's time. But it goes by too quick."

"I know, darlin'. I know all about it."

"I want to know everything about you. I don't want time to get away."

"Everything might be hard to swallow."

"I can handle it," I insist.

"It's not about you being able to handle it, it's about me being able to handle it."

"All right, I can buy that. But, Jesse," I say and sit up. "You don't have to handle it alone."

He reaches to the table and grabs Whitman. He hurls a quote about indignity and abuse, about rivers of tears, about looking on your own crucifixion and bloody crowning.

He doesn't know it yet, but I've come to this battle trained. I turn the page to a quote I've almost memorized, and read with as much conviction as the poet himself:

I do not ask who you are, that is not important to me,
You can do nothing and be nothing but what I will
    infold you...
On his right cheek I put the family kiss,
And in my soul I swear I never will deny him.

10-in-1 sideshow
ten carnival freak shows in the same tent for the price of one

Everything around us is silent, the room, the bar, the world. I hold Jesse's head against my chest for hours, it seems, before his voice slashes the silence. Bypassing my ears, his words, like heroin, shoot through my skin and go directly into my veins, where they're released into the bloodstream, so I get the full, immediate effect of his emotions. He hides his face as he talks, because after years of childhood infusions, shame flows through his veins.

Jesse weaves me in and out of his story and I suffer through his experiences as if they're just now happening, because he and I have done the unimaginable. We've redefined pregnancy; while I travel the painful barbed wire fence of his existence, he's curled safely inside my womb. The umbilical cord that ties him to me offers him the protection and support he needs to get through this experience again.

Jesse's story doesn't seem real. I didn't know places like that really existed, believing them to be strictly Hollywood inventions. I didn't know people like him really existed, other than in meaty carnival sideshows. But I have to believe because he's here, and the scars from his battles support his claims. I cry when he cries, I'm afraid when he's afraid. From time to time, I have to make myself remember that he's survived, that he's no longer there, that he has become a success story in his own right. He found a way to block the years out, flashing back only when something triggered his memory.

I feel like Alice let loose in a world of abstractions, unable to touch anything concrete, unsure which path will lead me out. It's said that in the midst of a nightmare where we're falling and falling, we awaken before we hit, saving ourselves from a real death. When it's time, Jesse breaks through the placenta that has kept him alive, and steps outside of me. Releasing himself from safety, he takes hold of one of my hands and then the other so as to pull me out of the danger that is him before I make contact with the ground.

My body is drained, and though Jesse's body feels tranquil, I know it's spent. My mind shuffles through his words, rearranges them, translates them until I can make sense out of them. It takes a while. Before he falls asleep, I tell him that in a few hours I'm due to make a run. I'm lying, but he doesn't know that. He moans inside. It rumbles against my hands like thunder.

"I'll be back," I say. "It's difficult, I know, but trust me."

"You won't come back."

There's not even an ounce of faith left in him. Like a slaughtered animal, he's been gutted and upended to bleed out. Before I can fill him again and sew him up, I have to explore his past, discover my resources. He's come without instructions, and I've come without experience.

For now, all I have is words, so I quote the only line of Whitman I've nearly memorized, again. I feel him smile against my skin. I think he's proud of my ability and desire to memorize poetry. He strikes back with a quote about faithful and friendly arms helping him.

And there it is. He's given in a little. He looks up at me to seal the commitment. Can I trust you, his eyes ask, locking into mine. Like ears against a safe, he slowly turns the combination, listening for the clicks, trying to break me open. I want to give him a better answer, but I can't help but think about my track record. What if I fail him, I ask myself, and that's when my eyes say to him, Not yet, not yet.

Now all his doubt has come back, crawling upon its belly like a dark shadow, across miles of barren, hostile states, across years of painstakingly cultivated self-confidence; it moves as stealthily as an intruder, hacking away at whatever little self-worth he's managed to assemble over the past twenty years.

My faithful, friendly arms are about to invite the enemy in.

❧

Trust Jesus. Trust Jesus. Trust Jesus.

It's a declaration that's painted on bridge abutments—next to overhead clearance warnings—all the way from South Carolina to Alabama. I've driven to Alabama because it's where Jesse's from; it's where his whole story takes place. I will never admit this to him but I'm confused and unsettled about what I've been told, and I need to see things for myself. Yet no matter how flustered I am, no matter how much I need to understand, I won't run away, and I won't betray his trust in me.

I move farther southwest into what Jesse referred to as Religionville.

"You mean the heart of the Bible Belt," I had corrected.

"No, I mean the bowels of the Bible Belt, because it's too fanatic for even the most religious, charismatic zealot to believe," he'd said with more anger in his voice than I'd ever heard.

Jesse has some earnest convictions about this; I'll never challenge them.

I've gotten a rental car—I can't do my detecting in a tractor trailer and expect not to be noticed—and a motel room. I ask if there's a bible in the room. The clerk stares at me as though I've asked him if the rooms have toilets; by the looks of things, that's questionable too.

The roads I follow, which pass by plush green farms, pastures of cows and horses, and rolling landscapes, become more vacant once I exit the highway. They become gravel paths and then tire tracks embedded in grass. The only animals I see are mangy dogs, or an occasional rooster. There are few signs of life down these paths, and it makes me wary. I travel from memory. His and now mine. I'm positive I'm on the right route. The landmarks are too fantastic to miss. There are confederate flags, of course, but they're nothing new; as a driver, they're the most common landmark one sees in the southern part of the country. The signs are something altogether different, though. One wedged in a field, surrounded by nothing, reads Have you been baptized in the spirit of the Holy Ghost?

The next, painted on the side of an old, run-down, window-shattered, weather-beaten barn says, For misery does not come from the earth, nor does trouble sprout from the ground; but human beings are born to trouble just as sparks fly upwards—Job 5:6–7

And another still: …the gift of speaking in strange tongues is proof for unbelievers…—1 Cor. 14:22–23

The hairs on my arms rise. I'm afraid I've gotten myself in deeper than I'll be able to handle; an even bigger fear is that I'll be snatched up and then offered as a sacrifice. But I think of Jesse, of the secrets we've shared, so I go on. I take a left at the old gas station—with its one remaining gas pump, its caved-in garage, stack of old tires, car bumpers—and travel two miles down before I spot the 1958 Ford truck that has a tree growing through its bed. There's a dirt road to the left of that, but it's easy to miss if you don't see the remains of a double-wide, just barely peeking out of the brush, split nearly in two by a tree limb. It's unbelievably comical, inconceivably the same as it was twenty-some years ago. It's exactly the way he described it, when he was once a part of it. It's hard to believe that someone as intelligent as Jesse, someone as beautiful and clean as he, was born and bred in such self-induced filth.

The more I scope out the area, the more nervous and sick to my stomach I become. During my days on the road, I've had to rent grubby motel rooms, merely for a shower, or even a few hours of privacy, but I knew there was nothing permanent about it. These conditions, though, are more than bad choices; they're a way of life, and it scares me to think that they're acceptable. I come upon the decrepit shack that was once his house. Who knows whose it is now. There are the woods that border it, an old privy hopefully not still functional, a barn with what appear to be shotgun holes through it, and a stack of bicycles, rusted through. That's where the path was, still is. I envision the times Jesse was dragged out of the house (his brothers went willingly) and down the path by a demented father, so that they could find some defenseless girl and have sex with her.

I allow myself a few deep breaths before cutting the engine and carefully getting out of the car. I don't move, though, because I can't stop staring at the conditions around me. I suspect that's why a woman comes out to the porch, her house dress dirty and torn, her hair matted and greasy.

"What you want?" she calls. She's in her sixties, and as skinny as a pencil drawing. Her cheeks are sunken, her skin as wrinkled as a woman in her eighties. She looks as if she's spent most of her life starved.

I take a step toward her. She backs up and moves to the side. One more step and we'll begin circling each other like animals.

"Are you Sarah Reid?" I ask, timidly.

"Who wants to know?" She narrows her eyes, and I notice how sharp they are, as though they're the only things on her that haven't aged.

Good question. Don't answer.

"I was told you're…" I have to think fast. A good cook? Impossible to believe. An excellent housekeeper? Clearly not. "I was told you're…"

"You ain't from around here."

I shake my head no.

"I need directions," I say.

She steps forward. There's a gleam of madness in her eye. She's smiling. Most of her teeth are missing and what remain are black. Impossible, I think again. This is 1996. Then I think about what Bobby once said, "You're liable to see just about everything there is to see," but who would've imagined this.

"You lookin' for the church," she hisses softly. Her smile deepens. Maddens.

No, I think.

Close your mouth, I beg.

Excuse yourself and leave, I plead to myself.

"Yes," I say.

"You with the authorities?"

I shake my head no. She's got her eyes narrowed at me, like she's looking through a spy glass.

"The newspapers?"

No, no, no; just the sane world. Okay, but who am I to talk, really?

"You come back here at five. You see that path down there? Drive right down there. You'll see other cars. Park and then follow the path on foot. Don't drive your car there, you understand me?"

She turns to leave but then comes back.

"I reckon you the first that's comin'. I hear it was in them city papers. I don't know who, but someone found out. We moved it so no one'll find it. How'd you hear about it if you ain't from the papers?"

Not from Jesse. Not your offspring. Not the child you never loved.

"From Brother..." I'm trying to think of the name Jesse mentioned. "He has the, um..." I indicate something on my face.

"The birthmark," she says quickly.

"Yes," I peep.

"That's Brother Jimmy Brown."

I snap my fingers like she's just stirred my terrible memory. "A man I know knows Brother Jimmy Brown. He's the one who sent me. He gave me your name. He said you could help."

"All right, you understand what I tole you. You come alone."

Before she asks for my promise in blood, I get into the car and drive back to the motel to shower. Everything about her makes me feel soiled and uneasy.

It's the first time I've entered a library outside my formal education. This one's a tiny, three-room building that cannot boast of having much in the way of good reading. But I'm not here for the literature, I'm here for the newspapers.

The librarian shows me to the most recent periodicals, retrieves the newspapers I request, and even teaches me how to use the copier. I find what I'm looking for on the front cover of the fourth paper.

"Do Miracles Really Exist?" the headline reads. Below it is a picture of a free-standing ceramic statue of the Virgin Mary that allegedly cries.

I put the paper down and rub my face.

In general, I'm baffled by religion. Kneeling and praying to something you can't see. Asking for strength and putting faith and money in something that is visually nonexistent. I ask the same question so many other atheists and skeptics ask: Where is this God when people suffer from hunger, or disease, or car crashes?

Agnes as a Catholic, Bobby as a Greek Orthodox, Gary as a Baptist, a trucker friend, Johnny J, as a Methodist. What confuses me is the basis of their beliefs. God, or Jesus, or the trinity of the holy spirit. One kneels, one doesn't. One takes communion, or drinks wine, or poison. They call each other sinners and misguided...so who's right?

Then Jesse came along and added to the pile of confusion. He tried to be very specific, very simple for my sake. His eyes flatten when he talks about religion. He knows the bible like he knows the spread of his body. He could spend the rest of his entire verbal life quoting from it when he communicates. But, like people, religion failed him. He grew to resent it, replaced the bible passages with Whitman, and began life all over again.

The religion started with the Evangelists, Jesse said, and then some divided to become Charismatics; from them came the snake handlers, or the Holy Ghost People. They weren't a bad group. Serious, but friendly. They were zealous, but accepting. All the groups were independent of one another. The only thing they had in common was their literal interpretation of the bible, but each group emphasized its own passage of the scripture. The first group of Holy Ghost People his mother worshipped with was good, low-to middle-income, working-class people. They taught their worshipers to be merciful and loving. They helped each other. They cared about Jesse as though he were their own.

It didn't get bad until he was five. It was around that time his mother and her sister, and several others, branched off. This new group met at each other's pole barns and sheds. Well, everyone's but Jesse's. His father told his mother that if they so much as drove by, he'd shoot each and every one of them dead on the spot. Like so many others, he was prejudiced against people who drank strychnine to test their faith in God. Strangers calling them "holy rollers" was derogatory, but it got worse when his mother and her group formed their own subset. This new group wasn't like the other snake handlers. They weren't merciful and loving. Vile and frightening, they went against everything the other holy ghost groups preached. From the very beginning they knew about Jesse, they believed he was the devil, and this small group of people kept his disfigurement a secret. They determined he wasn't the miracle I see him as. I didn't know what they saw him as, until I was there with them, seeing with my own eyes their statue weep, listening with my own ears to them condemn "the beast with ten horns and seven heads that cursed God and that came out of the sea." No, they didn't see him as a miracle, they saw him as the one who was let loose out of prison after a thousand years, who now goes forth and tries to deceive the world.

I park my small, rented Taurus next to a 1979 Ford station wagon with front quarter-panels that have been pieced together from parts of other cars. There are at least twenty other automobiles parked around the gravel lot, not one of them new or even close to it, but I'm the only body standing in this totally isolated area.

I cringe at the sound of my boots crunching down on the stone, and am grateful, for a few brief steps, for the soft wet grass that leads to the path. I make my way slowly across the cracking twigs, toward what appears to be a building that has been fashioned together—much like the station wagon—with boards from an old house and a pole barn. It is even more isolated than the lot, fully surrounded by acres and acres of woods. I'm aware that I'm on my own. No strategy, no back up plan. No one even knows I'm here, but I keep going because without this information, I won't know how to help out or win over Jesse.

As I approach the small building, two middle-aged women stand at the front door, and, like ushers at a wedding, hook their arms through mine, to lead me in. What twenty-eight years ago began as a small group of ten, has now grown to over fifty. Everyone greets each other similarly, with a quick kiss on the lips. The elderly sit on a bench along the back wall with a handful of women who cradle infants. The rest mingle in the center, and around the piano. A dirty young woman who looks like she could've once been a member of the Manson clan is banging a tambourine and dancing in a circle in the middle of the room. No one seems to even hear what I'm assuming is a song, though it sounds more like someone in miserable pain. I casually make my way toward the far wall, never looking anyone in the eye, but watching the movement, memorizing the faces, keeping my exits in sight. No one asks my name, or even touches me, but they nod as though expecting me. Perhaps Sarah Reid has told them I'd be here.

Standing by the dancing tambourine girl is a neatly dressed man with a thin goatee, his black hair slicked back like the way Jesse wears his.

His voice is thin, quiet, and he speaks to the floor. "I found the Holy Ghost when I was a boy. God helped take the evil out of me. He helped get me out of jail, and I promised him, I said to him that if he did, I'd spend my life serving him."

A few members move to the fold-out chairs around him and nod. Another woman, older than the girl singing, stands now too, and says, "I know that the Lord got me down on the floor and baptized me, halamaas halamaas...Glory be to God...I take it everywhere I can..." She jerks her neck in and out like a strutting rooster.

I look around to see if others find her babble confusing, but more have joined and have closed their eyes and move their mouths in prayer. At first, they're only mouthing their prayers, but then everyone starts chanting different things at once. It's loud and obnoxious and I want out.

My stomach turns and I back against the wall, pressing myself close to it. There's no direct way out of here. They've backed me in. As though I'm stuck to the wall, I try to drag my way across it, toward the exit.

Jesse's mother stands on a chair, closes her eyes, and holds her arms upward and hollers, "'Satan will bring them all together for battle, as many as the grains of sand on the seashore.'"

"Oh yes. Amen. Praise be," they agree one after the other.

"What we know is what we know," she chants, and then begins to shake. "What we saw is what we saw. We have to find what was lost to us. We need to find what we lost and throw it into the lake of fire and sulfur where it will be tormented every day and every night until the end of time!"

Sarah Reid, whose frenzied weeping seems blasphemous in the same room as the statue with Mary's woeful stare, proclaims quickly, "The Holy Ghost moved upon me." The others now have their arms up in the air, they sway, they mumble their *praise Gods* and *glory bes* and *oh mys* as she talks. "The Holy Ghost tole me what I was supposed to do. I thought it was done to me because of what *I* did."

"Not you, Sister Sarah," a female voice calls from the circle. "You done *nothin'* wrong. *Nothin'* but pray to Jesus. *Nothin'* but set your life and love and heart to defeating the devil."

"I won't ask you to pray for me," Sarah calls and falls to her knees.

"Glory God, praise be."

"I won't ask you to pray for me, but I'll ask you to help me undo what been done to me."

Now they fall to their knees, heads together, palms up toward the ceiling.

"I knowed when it was happening," she continues. "I felt the devil seep into me when he done his deed. I felt the thorns of the devil move through my body and ripen, and when it come out, oh Lord, praise be, we seen the devil with our own eyes."

Jesse's mother talks of his inception and her pregnancy candidly. It appears to be a story any one of these people could tell, they've heard it so often that I wonder if she tells it for my benefit, so I'll know what my future religious purpose is to be. To understand how evil Jesse is. To hunt him down and deliver him to them. When it occurs to me that she may want me to know everything, my insides tremor from fear, but more, I think from anger. Every last cell in my body wants to tear out of here, but I can't. I can't. Not until I know.

When Jesse's mother first realized she was pregnant, she tried to abort him two times, once using a stick from the woods. Her sister took her to a man who claimed to be a spiritual doctor. He put his dirty hands inside her and found that her last attempt was unsuccessful. He told the sister to gather some women from the church group, women she trusted, women who truly believed the devil was inside Sarah Reid. An hour later she came back with three women and the doctor arrived with two other "spiritual" men. They stripped off her clothes and shackled her, arms out, legs spread, to a wooden platform. If the devil could not be extracted with objects, they would use the semen of holy men to poison it. While the women sat around her and prayed, the three men gave her the best spiritual fucking she ever had.

At the end of her pregnancy, Jesse's father nearly beat her to death because she was spending so much time with the church people. She went into an early labor and, because the doctor couldn't be tracked down, her sister, who had never delivered a baby before, was forced to call upon a neighbor, who was not particularly fond of Sarah Reid, to help. If only the spiritual doctor had been available, Jesse's mother and aunt lamented, only the three of them would've seen the baby, and he surely would have smothered Jesse before he'd have taken his first breath and rid the world of something so evil and shameful.

Jesse's differences didn't become apparent until he was just over a year old. Sarah took her sister aside and the two tried to figure out ways to keep Jesse's father and brothers from finding out. He'd kill her first, and then the baby, they knew, so whenever they were around, Jesse was whisked away, and left at his aunt's house.

Do miracles really exist?

Before me the statue of Mary weeps tears. While the group plays instruments, or convulses on the floor, or sways back and forth, I approach the table she rests upon and wait for something to happen.

She stands no more than a foot-and-a-half tall. Two much larger statues, one of Joseph and another of Mary holding the baby Jesus, tower over her from behind. She is dwarfed by these two bronze sculptures, which are laced with flowers, but not by small Mary. The only bit of her ceramic body that has color is the veil, which is blue and cascades with carefully molded ripples down her body. Her hands are pressed together in prayer, her head is tilted sideways, her downward gaze is mournful. The sorrowful expression on her face is so realistic, I'm jolted to the core when, I swear, her eyes follow me when I take a step sideways.

I raise my hand to get someone to come over to me, but they're too busy to even pay the slightest bit of attention to me or Mary. Tiny tears slide down her face one drop at a time. They aren't consistent, but occasional, and still frequent enough to keep me standing there. When I feel certain no one is looking, I let a tear drip onto my finger, and taste it. It is no more or less salty than my own. Impossible. I poke around and under Mary, looking for a tube, or an electrical wire, or a reservoir: something to show that these people, who aren't smart enough to know when they're being raped and exploited, have somehow rigged the statue. I'm afraid to admit to myself that there isn't anything, that it's real and that's why they've hidden it.

What should I do? I'd get down on my knees and pray, but I don't know how. The other option is to leave, but I can't because I'm yanked into the center of the circle of praying people. They press their bodies against me. They vibrate their bodies against

me. Their language is muffled. Between their praises come gut-
tural sounds and words that are either filled with all consonants
or all vowels. I'm afraid of being trampled, I'm afraid that their
speaking in tongues will make sense to me. Their hands grope
me the way Jesse had once described them groping him. At
first, I slap their hands away, but they're persistent and they
won't let me out. I resign myself to the fact that I'm going to
go through his experiences firsthand.

Jesse had told me that between the ages of one and five, it
was easy for his mother and aunt to keep his disfigurement a
secret from his father and brothers because they were never
around. While it was true that his mother wished he had never
been born, she didn't want her husband to be the one to get rid
of him because he'd kill her too; plus, she wanted to keep that
honor for herself. First, she would offer him up to the Father.
He would give the worshipers a sign to show how to deal with
Jesse. She hinted to the others in the group that something was
wrong with him, but when they held or played with Jesse all
they saw was a little boy desperate for love and attention.

They began to get weary of his mother, of the way she
violently spoke in tongues and pushed Jesse around. Some
approached her because they didn't understand what Jesse
could have done to upset her to the point that she obviously
hated him. They offered to take him away for a while, give her
a chance to get her home life together, but she refused. As far
as she was concerned, even the Lord wouldn't take Jesse, so she
made her move.

She, her sister, and the others who witnessed her "cleansing"
began gathering for their own private services. The first few
were spent establishing the ways in which the meetings would
be run, mostly by the spiritual doctor. As time went on, though,
the meetings began to focus more and more on Jesse. They
took off his clothes and displayed him on the table.

"You see what evil looks like," the doctor said to the congregation, pushing a staff between Jesse's legs. "The serpent takes
many shapes."

One night after a meeting, when Jesse was seven, and his father had been gone for days, drinking, his brothers presumably with him, she and her sister put a dog chain around Jesse's neck and chained him, naked, to a hook in the wall. They put bowls of food and water just beyond his reach, and there he lay in urine and excrement and vomit and blood.

It's hard to believe it could, but it got worse.

They grope me in ways that are perverse. I can't help but feel like I'm in the center of an orgy, but I'm afraid to open my eyes to look. I don't want to see what's being done to me, what was done to Jesse. If I look, I'll leave, and if I leave, I'll never truly understand what Jesse went through, and I won't be able to help him. Their praises and moans continue so loudly they drown out the guitar and tambourine. After a while there is one sound that overpowers their voices, but it's a quiet noise, a low-key presence that gradually becomes larger and larger.

Hands fall off me, people step away, the mumbles grow quiet, the rattles at my feet grow loud. Sarah and her sister carry over the wooden table that Jesse was once strapped to. Two women dance around it with five-foot rattlers in their hands.

"If I die from a snake bite, it's God's will," one says.

"Praise be," the other answers.

"Come up and declare your love before Jesus Christ our savior," Sarah Reid says to me.

"Embrace God," her sister says, "take your salvation cocktail." Someone hands me a cup filled with a fluid that must be the strychnine Jesse told me about.

"It's God's will," someone says. It may have been me. I don't actually drink the strychnine. Instead, I pass it to a woman who is standing to my side, with her arm around my waist. Slipping a pill between my lips, she closes my mouth until she sees me swallow it. I do, I have. It splashes into my stomach, and fearfully, I wait to feel its effects

"God's will," she hisses in my ear.

Close your eyes, I tell myself, but the action may have been misinterpreted. Someone says something like, "That's right, close your eyes and give yourself up to the Lord. If you ain't got the Holy Ghost, come get it. You need it, you want it. Amen."

"It is time our sister is baptized with the holy spirit," one of the men says.

Two people wrap my arms around their shoulders and nearly have to drag me as we follow a procession out of the church and through the woods. Every time my head falls backward, someone lifts it and tells me to rejoice in God's world. The path through the woods to the river is dark and I have no idea where we are, or how to get out if I have a chance. The arthritic-looking tree limbs seem to wave me forward, and I'm afraid of what's ahead.

Without warning my legs are wet up to my knees. I'm not standing on my own, and, tripping forward, I try to brace myself, but my arm penetrates the calm water. Before I go all the way under, I'm lifted by a man who puts one arm around my stomach and the other around my neck. A man and a woman stand on either side of him, and nod as he tells them his first allegiance is to God. Water snakes slither across the top of the water, but no one notices other than me. We walk over the muck, through the weeds, past lily pads. Snakes continue to glide by, making swirls around our thighs, as we walk deeper into the water.

I'm afraid, I say. It was the same thing Jesse had once told them, but they never listened. I hate snakes, I say, as Jesse, who is violently afraid of snakes, once had told them, but these people never listen. The hand on my shoulder pushes me to my knees, so that the water is now at my chest level. I know what's going to happen because Jesse described every detail he could recall. The hand on the back of Jesse's head that gripped him by the hair and shoved him under now does the same thing to me.

Struggling to come up, I gulp in a mouthful of water and throw it up when I'm pulled out. There's barely enough time to take another breath before I'm shoved under again. Snakes whirl around my head, weeds stroke my cheeks. I begin to struggle again. They drag me up when they're ready. Not a second sooner.

"Give your life to God," they say, before dunking me under for a third time.

Jesse was too tired to fight, and so am I. He said it was easier to let go, to give up, and hope that they'd stop. I'll do the same thing. Sound slows down under water. Acting as a cushion, it alters any pitch that's biting, funnels the noise and releases it under the surface as dull. It would seem impossible to comprehend what they're saying from above me, but while I'm under, I have time to wait for the syllables, the accents, to catch up to one another.

"This is a new level of communicating with the lord," I hear from beneath the water.

Keep holding, I think to myself, but I feel myself starting to black out. My body must go slack. I'm not sure. I'm too busy listening to the weeds talk to each other. We've seen this before, they say, before assuring me that it's not the end of my life. They remind me that when they knew one more immersion would have killed Jesse, the doctor dragged him back to the barn, strapped him again to the table and forced himself into Jesse as far as he could. I wonder if that is what they're going to do to me, now. Maybe drowning is a better end.

They prayed around Jesse, his mother, his aunt, the others, while they ravaged him. Sometimes the men penetrated Jesse, sometimes the women used a staff, sometimes even a thorny crown was put upon his head. All for Jesse's pain and their pleasure. It usually wound down when someone vomited up their poison or got bitten by a snake, and it always ended with the doctor whispering in Jesse's ear, "Let the Lord do your doctorin'."

Never, Jesse'd think, but then his brothers found out about him, after his mother had left him chained naked to the wall and saw what he was made of. They beat him but never told their father because he surely would have killed Jesse, and then what would they do for fun. And every time they'd come to him,

Jesse'd repeat to himself until it was over, "I'm letting the Lord do my doctoring."

I awaken in a damp motel bed. I have scratches down my arms and around my cheeks. My thighs have bruises on them, finger marks, it looks like. I'm even sore between my legs, and I know exactly what happened. I remember watching them take turns, but I don't remember fighting them off.

I dare to glance in the mirror and see that I look like, well, like I've seen a ghost, I decide. I take a shower, drink coffee, and smoke cigarettes. I check out, find a bar, gulp down three shots of Jack, and smoke until my body stops trembling. I'd gladly go through it all over again if it meant making Jesse's memories disappear. His words are still in my head, and their handprints linger on my body.

What's left to do but go back to South Carolina? The 120 sign is ahead, but instead of taking it, I turn around and go back to Sarah Reid's house. I must be as mad as she is.

She doesn't come out this time, so I have to go up on the porch and knock. I peek in the window to the family room and envision Jesse chained there like an animal. Sarah Reid comes to the door. We stare at each other. I make myself not see her in Jesse, make myself see the abusive monster she is. I want to pound her with my fists, want to see her bleed, make her suffer the way she made him suffer—me suffer.

"What you want?" she asks, and that's when I step forward to hit her.

She must know by my face. My jaw aches with tension from holding back the vulgar words desperate to attack her.

You whore! I want to scream. You fucking vile psychotic whore!

I could tear her heart out in rage.

"You come back for more?" There is the slightest hint of a smirk.

I calm myself down. I say softly, "I want to tell you that you..." what? I think to myself.

"That I what?" she mocks.

That you should have been a mother to the child you gave birth to, that you should have worshiped Jesse instead of your snakes, that Jesse deserved better; better than you, you loathsome white trash.

"Nothing," I say, and climb down the steps, sensing that she follows me.

"You seen him, ain't you?" she hisses in excitement and disbelief.

Don't deny him, I say to myself. But she doesn't deserve to hear of his successes. She doesn't deserve you, Jesse. I stare at her and through her. I stare around her and inside of her. I force myself to see every last filthy ounce of her so I'll always remember.

"You haven't gained the right to know what I know."

I, for one, believe in miracles.

I come home to Jesse like I said I would, but I stand by the front door of the bar and watch for a while before I approach him. He's sitting on his bar stool, chain smoking. His hand shakes every time he raises it to his mouth. He stares into the distance, I imagine, wondering where I am, or if I'm coming back, or if I'm sorry I've gotten myself involved with such a freak. That's what he would be thinking. But I'm thinking my heart is ready to explode because of what I feel for him. I take only one step closer before he glances up and sees me. He slides off the stool and goes toward his room. I follow.

He's leaning up against the dresser, waiting to see if I've come to say goodbye.

I stand in the doorway.

He looks away in shame. He's protected himself from exposure for so long, covered up his secrets for so long, that opening them up again has brought back all the insecurities.

I stare at him and try to come up with something to say. But I've come back with so much experience that I realize I don't need words; he doesn't need words. What he needs are my arms, my acceptance, maybe my shoulder. I walk right up to him and pull him into me, soothing him as gently as I can. This time it isn't sexual, it's maternal, and though I feel protective, at first, I'm afraid it's not going to be enough to save him. I suddenly wish I were a superhero and that I could fly up in the sky to carry him down safely. Instead, it's as if I'm on the ground, running in circles with my arms extended, trying to determine what factor the wind will play when he drops.

My arms tighten and when Jesse responds it occurs to me that neither of us needs to speak now. Because with every word Jesse's spoken, with every truth I've experienced, we've inched farther and farther out on a tree limb where we hover above roof tops and skyscrapers and clouds. There's only so much farther out we can go before the weight of our entire lives eventually breaks it. With every word he's spoken and with every truth I've experienced, the weight of it all is about to send us plummeting.

We can't hide from it, Jesse. We've nearly reached the point of no return; but at least when we go, we'll go together.

anima and animus
female aspects of a man and male aspects of a woman

"Come with me," I say.

The idea hits my brain like rain on a dry ground.

Jesse is curled against my body, on the bed. My hand is cupped around a heaving stomach. I'm not allowed to move it in either direction.

"It's too complicated."

"Bullshit. If you don't want to go with me, say so. Don't try to pretend it's something else."

Jesse turns his head to look at me. "Where will I sleep and shower?"

"This isn't high school gym class," I say. "The showers are private. We can share the bed in the sleeper or get separate motel rooms, if you prefer. I promise I won't touch you."

"It's not that I don't want you to…" Jesse begins. I've heard this at least a hundred times now.

"I know, Jesse. What I mean is, you'll be in charge. It'll be fun."

"Fun," Jesse repeats. "I haven't had fun since, well, since I met you."

"Will Gary be okay with it?"

"Gary? Well, sure, *he'll* be fine."

The sentence ends, but it sounds incomplete. It sounds like he's thinking, But will I?

Our travels take us from state to state. From coast to coast. At first Jesse is uncertain, uncomfortable. Like a dog that's been beaten nearly to death, he sits in the passenger seat with his legs either curled beneath him or up against his chest as though he's trying to tuck himself away from the world. It takes a little coaxing to get him out of his shell, to make him see there's a place for him in this world as much as for anyone else. That he's better than every man or woman I've ever known and cared for.

Words are a dime a dozen. We shoot them out with our spit. We've got a great reserve, and our minds and bodies will always produce more. An old boyfriend showed me how unconvincing words were. I answered every one of his carefully chosen expressions of love with a throwaway catch phrase: *yeah, me too.*

"I really want this to work."

"Yeah, me too."

"I can't help but think about the future."

"Yeah, me too."

After a while, he caught on. He got smart and backed me into a corner.

"You tell me," he said, "but you never show me."

Yes, he wanted to hear me say the words, but even more he wanted to see it in my eyes, my body language. He thought he had the power, and the right kiss, to awaken his fairy-tale sleeping beauty. Like his imaginary princess, I had a fine set of lips, trim long legs, a flat belly. But I had no heart. He didn't need lips to awaken me, he needed a defibrillator.

I couldn't give him the words he wanted. Nor would I let him, not even once, hold me at night. Why was that so damn important to men? What I did instead was give him a well-executed blowjob. No complaints when he was on his back squirming, but the anger rose with his replenishing fluids.

If he had said something like, "I feel like this whole mating process is ridiculously overrated," I would have bellowed, "I love you, baby!"

Words are weak. There has to be another way to show Jesse that my life would be different without him in it. The only way I can think of is through silence. It's what Jesse has always been most comfortable with. I'm hoping his silence will reveal to me how to show him he's not like any of the others I've been with.

With each day he offers a little more personal conversation, and unfurls his body, one small piece at a time. On the seventh day, he calls Gary, and I put in my dutiful call to Agnes, to see how things are. Agnes's only complaint is that her dentures fell apart so she's been gumming her food. No smart comments, no grievances, no begging. For a second, I'm thrown a curve ball; in all the years I've known her, she's never been satisfied. She asks me if I've sent out her weekly package, which I have, and tells me to be careful. Not, Come back home, or Have you had enough of that nonsense, but Be careful. I feel suddenly useless.

Gary reports that everything is running smoothly. He tells Jesse to relax and have a good time. So, we've both been cast off by our dependents, and are left to believe that people can get along just fine without us.

Then Jesse does the most remarkable thing, and I assume he does it because he's so thrown off guard. He takes off his flannel shirt. His T-shirt underneath is bleach white, crisp, without wrinkles. This is showing, not telling. Jesse has never let me, or anyone, see even the smallest portion of his sun depleted white skin. He has always worn a flannel shirt over his T-shirt. He's never exposed himself in public.

But Jesse seems to have stripped without even realizing he's done so. He says, "If it weren't for Gary, I just don't know. That man has been my right arm from day one, I swear it."

I swallow, glancing nervously. I'm finally going to bring it up because Jesse now sits comfortably, almost languidly, in the seat next to me.

"Does he know?" I ask timidly. I think I already know the answer.

"Does he know what?" Jesse challenges.

Does he honestly not know what I'm talking about, or does he want me to say it? I always fail these little tests.

"About you?"

Jesse scratches his elbow. His skin craves sun, the hair is fine. When I reach out and rub my hand down his arm, goosebumps rise. His initial reaction is to pull away, but he forces himself to relax. Learning to function outside of his habitat is so hard to do. I don't want to make him uncomfortable, so I move my hand into his and clasp his fingers as tight as I can.

"Does he know that I'm a monster?"

"Don't, Jesse."

"An aberration. A disfigured failure."

"Stop it!" I yell and he closes his mouth as firmly as he shot out the words.

He's defensive and I'm frightened. It is better to stay quiet and breathe and smoke and drink coffee. And so much easier.

"I've always wanted to see the inside of one of those," Jesse says.

I follow his finger.

"The guys call them big tits," I say, referring to the salt shed.

"That's appropriate, I reckon, for a bunch of over-sexed men. Must get a lot of use up north."

"Oh yeah."

"What?" Jesse asks.

I shake my head, but he won't stop looking at me. I give in. I always give in to Jesse. It's hard not to when I've got a bit in my mouth.

"It goes like this," I tell Jesse:

"Once upon a time there was a vulgar man named Dennis Lutz. I hated him and he hated me. It was uncanny but somehow, he found women to have sex with him. A lot of women and a lot of sex. It has nothing to do with our hating each other but it's a notable fact. One day—"

"Hold on. Why are your stories about him always sexual?"

"This one has to do with the salt shed. It seems fitting, since that's what we're talking about."

"There has to be something good about him. We're all vulnerable in one way or other, Danny, even villains."

"I love that you're such a staunch supporter of the underdog, Jesse, I really do," I say, smirking, and Jesse gives me a friendly slap on the thigh. "All right, I'll begin the story from an earlier point. The day before.

"One day a co-worker, Vic, asked me if I'd help get his '62 Beetle running, which I was glad to do because I hadn't been working on cars much. Agnes and the house kept me fairly busy—and that's a story in itself because Agnes was trying to set me up with the grandson of one of her friends, an accountant who made me crazy with his manners, always opening the door for me, pecking me on the cheek after our first date, such sexist horse shit when all I wanted was to get laid because it had been months since I had. After my third date with this clown, I was so desperate I nearly called Pip for a quick romp but I was too embarrassed to let him into my apartment because we had celebrated Valentine's Day just the week before and the accountant sent me a dozen roses, a ridiculously large heart-shaped box of candy, and a white teddy bear holding a red heart—"

"That's sweet. What's wrong with that?"

I roll my eyes, then blow my air horn for some kids in a station wagon.

"Come on, Jesse. I wasn't looking for a permanent love affair. I wanted a hand other than my own touching me."

"What was your boyfriend's name?"

I snort at the reference. "Romeo," I quip.

"Nice. So, you slept with this Pip guy because your Romeo was a gentleman. You've mentioned Pip several times. Should I be jealous?"

"Pip. Good-looking guy. Real muscular. Not my type but deliciously hard pecs. No, I didn't sleep with him then, but I did sleep with him after I quit. That's not the point. The point is Romeo was too attached to his etiquette. When we went out, I wore jeans, and he wore his suit and tie."

"So what?"

"We went to the fucking bowling alley, Jesse!" I laugh.

"Well, did it come to fruition?"

"What the hell does that mean?"

"Did he fulfill your horny needs?"

I laugh again. Words like that sound so ill-fitting coming out of Jesse's mouth.

"I'm going to tell you the truth, though it'll seem like a load of bullshit. The guy was a virgin. He'd never slept with anyone in his entire life."

Jesse's cheeks redden and he looks down. The cigarette in my mouth falls into my lap. I grab for it and Jesse pats my smoking crotch. If I weren't on fire, the gesture would have turned me on. We don't talk and I pull into the next rest area.

"I'm sorry. I was just trying to—"

"Don't, Danny. It's fine. I'm fine."

I sigh. "I guess I just don't know how you can keep yourself from feeling horny."

"I have this motto: it's okay to read the menu, as long as you don't order."

Cruel advice for a starving man.

"Was I on your menu?" I can't help asking.

Jesse smiles a little. "Breakfast, lunch, and dinner."

I smile back. "No dessert or snacks?"

"I do have a waistline to watch," Jesse says.

"Why? You having one of those southern Debutante Balls?"

Jesse laughs. "Well hell, there wouldn't be anyone there to court me."

"I would," I say seriously. Jesse smiles softly. I'm beginning to think I'll never be able to live without seeing that small perfectly outlined smile every day. "I am sorry."

"I told you I'm fine."

"Prove it."

Jesse, who only twice since that night in his room has taken the initiative to kiss me, who always waits for me to make a move, leans over, cups a hand around my neck, and draws me to his lips. Those kisses are too dangerous for a woman whose biggest concern has been when and where her first orgasm from Jesse will come from.

"Why are we sitting here?" Jesse asks, as though trying to pretend he hasn't just asserted himself in that manner. "Come on, sugar, we've got a load to deliver. And I want to hear the rest of your story."

I lie and say, "I don't remember what I was saying."

"He was a virgin, and I imagine you taught him a thing or two about how easily the body contorts."

"Some people marvel at my skills to bring them pleasure," I say.

"I don't doubt that," Jesse mumbles. "How long did it take before he finally made a move?"

"He didn't. It was probably our eighth date when I asked him if he didn't just want to sleep together, and you know what he said? He wanted to remain a virgin till he got married."

"What did you do?"

"I laughed. Not at him, but at the idea that he thought I was a virgin. So I said, 'You do realize I'm not a virgin, right?' You'd have thought I'd just confessed to being a serial rapist. Needless to say, he never called me again."

"Didn't that hurt your feelings?"

"Hell no, pissed me off a little. I mean, I sat through hours of his boring tax stories, he could have at least gotten me off once." Jesse stares at me wide-eyed, trying to figure out if I'm serious or not. I could go either way. "Anyway, this has nothing to do with Dennis."

"Maybe not directly, but I'd say there are certainly some similarities between you two."

Now I stare, wide-eyed. I would have taken less offense to being called a serial rapist.

"Keep up the insults and I'll dump your sorry ass at a chicken coop with a hungry smokey."

"Your threat is lost on me," Jesse says with an arrogant tone.

"It's a weigh station where lonely sheriffs sit and wait for fresh meat."

"All I'm saying, Danny, is that you ridicule Dennis for his sexual encounters, but you see yours as what's due to you. You see your date's virginity as comical, but my lack of experience as alluring."

"Whose side are you on?" I ask, trying to keep the edge out of my voice.

"It's hypocritical."

"Fuck you."

"Now there's no need to get testy."

"I'll get testy if I want to. I'll give you hypocritical," I mutter to myself.

Jesse doesn't know where that sentence is headed, and it really doesn't matter because it doesn't apply to him. If he were any other man, I'd lecture him on society's sexual double standard. How unacceptable and whorish it is that I, as a woman, choose to have casual sex, but how masculine and expected it is for men. But it'll be a point fallen on deaf ears so I keep quiet.

We ride in silence for hours. Because I don't know what to call what just happened, I don't know how to rectify it. It would be easier if we were at the bar. I could just leave and not come back. But then, I remind myself, I'd never see Jesse again and I would rather...

What? I ask myself. You would rather what?

I would rather go without sex than go without Jesse's friendship and kisses. That fact alone makes me realize exactly what Jesse means to me.

Suddenly the silence is treacherous. I'm half tempted to set my lap on fire again, just to get a knee jerk reaction. Anything. But Jesse is content with silence.

Without Jesse distracting me, I'm susceptible to the disturbances on the highway. When I'm defenseless like this, the fatalities rise like enormous balloons. Difficult not to notice. But I stubbornly refuse to give in to them. I force them aside by gripping the wheel tighter, and focusing so intently on the interstate before me, and nothing more, that my head aches and my eyes burn.

By 11:30, I'm exhausted, but I can't stop because Jesse's been in the sleeper for the past hour. By midnight I have to pull into a rest area. I can barely keep my eyes open, and the chances that the black dog'll be out searching for me are one hundred percent. He just takes you by surprise. You open your eyes and he's there. I think of Bobby succumbing to him and feel an ache in my heart. If I were alone, I'd allow myself a nice long cry, but I'm not. Before I can feel resentful of that, I think of Jesse in the sleeper. We may not be speaking, but I'm comforted by the fact that he's here.

I wince when the air brake hisses like an alarm, then I try to settle myself in the seat. But how can I sleep knowing Jesse is behind me, maybe awake and longing for me, or dreaming of ways to get back home and away from me?

I go for a walk. There are only three other trucks parked, their drivers resting. Two cars are dark and silent. There's only one foolish woman, confused and wandering in circles. I sit on a damp grassy knoll and then plop back to study the stars. Hundreds, millions, billions; they multiply as I lie there. I pick out the constellations, starting with the dippers because they're the easiest to find. I search for Jesse's Gemini. They're up there somewhere. What I hadn't thought of before was, there are two of Jesse already. I'm really just a tag along, getting in the way.

When I had gotten back from Alabama the only thing he told me was that I could think of him as defective, but I was not to feel sorry for him. But I thought to myself, he is in no way flawed. Jesse is a sense of completion. Doubled. A sister to his masculine side and a brother to his feminine side. His own soulmate. A sun and a moon, a new moon and a full moon; the entire world is in awe of his cycle. He is a dragon and a tiger.

On Jesse's midriff between his heart and belly button—the center point of his being he said—is a large tattoo of Yin and Yang. He showed it to me the night I returned. A good omen! I thought. I have the same thing, I announced excitedly, and lowered my waist band to reveal the pattern on my pelvic bone. But mine, I was reminded when I saw it again, is incomplete, though Jesse didn't think so. His isn't just a part of the whole, he is the whole.

Somewhere in the mass of stars, Gemini is up there holding Jesse's stories, looking down at me as I stare up and wonder.

Stars do twinkle. One gleams here, another answers from there.

It's as though there's a conversation going on that I'm not privy to. I'm both nosy and envious. The sky talks. I know it does. I heard it the day Dennis died and I hear it now. It's the sound of the sun and the clouds, the swish of air under birds' wings, balloons lost out of the hands of children, all of it, everything combined and filtered and then released again as what humans hear as silence. In the stillness of the night, the stars have their turn. They tell a story through the light they shed, the light they collected the past millions of years. In those twinkles is the tale of Jesse's life from ten years ago. If I can experience the past in the light that reflects from the stars, why can't I pluck one down, listen to a page of his history, and take some of the burden away from him?

I reach my hand up, close my eyes, and choose randomly. At first, it's hot, fiery hot, melting hot, but the longer I hold it, the more it cools, crackling like a sparkler in my hand, the heat easing until it's still.

Here I am, it says. But don't look at me. Promise you won't look.

I promise.

Just release yourself to me. Look into my center. The story is here, if you look deep enough. Meditate; let yourself sleep, if you can.

Will it be easier?

Just let yourself go and hear Jesse's story.

You have questions. Me too. I grew up with questions. Not the same kind as yours. Mine were too philosophical for a child. I didn't grow up running around yards, playing kick ball. I grew up inside a southern operating theater with people masked not in surgical gowns and gloves but with snakes and poison, and so many other hurtful things—poking and prodding abusing hurting shaming praying whipping penetrating.

I learned to disassociate but it took a while. I learned it from the girls my father and brothers brought to the woods.

The first time the "doctor" put the rounded end of the staff inside my vagina, I knew I was different, and I knew I was—what's the right word—unseemly. I had been fully exposed to the bodies of men and women. The only times I saw my father's and brothers' bodies was when their pants were down, penises erect, standing in line waiting their turn to do things to those helpless runaway girls. My father would always go first and he'd make us stand next to him so we could learn. I was six the first time I saw him do it. The way he spread her legs and there was nothing there, nothing sticking out. He placed the tip of his penis into the folds of her labia. She was fighting so hard, like her whole life depended on it. Two of my brothers held down her arms and the other her belly. He put himself in and pushed until she opened and I thought: that poor girl, so unlike me, and at the same time so like me. How was that possible?

The girls would scream, but then, it was as though some-thing, something spiritual came over them, the way they'd stare out at me, unfocused at first and then it was like they caught sight of something inside me, and I would think that maybe they'd caught sight of my soul, and it was somehow a source of strength. Then their eyes would glaze over and I knew they had found the strength of the Lord and the strength of the Lord was inside of me. Here was this amazing truth I came to believe in: not only was He helping them get through it, but so was I.

We went so often into the woods, into a shack they had built for this very purpose. It was a shrine. They put the girls on a table, a table just like the one in my mother's church. We were closer in spirit than they ever knew. I stood by their sides, pre-tending to hold down their arms, but I'd hold their hands and silently pray, and they'd grip me as if they were bearing a child, and they'd stare at that light in my eyes and I never ever looked away because looking away was the very same thing as taking away the power of the Holy Ghost.

You're wondering how I got around having intercourse with them. When I was young enough, I could run. My daddy would come after me with a belt and whip me till I could barely stand. He'd say, "You gon' start taking that pussy or I'm gon' kill you." He would have; of that I'm certain. If it wasn't him then it would have been my mama. They both despised my very existence, but for different reasons. My father had no idea what was hidden beneath my clothes. The only reason she kept that a secret was because he would have killed her too.

But early on, before they ever knew, I got smart. My brothers would masturbate while they were waiting their turns. So, I'd put my hand down my pants and pretend to do the same while I watched. It was all bad, but I had to save myself. When I was on my own table, and the doctor would penetrate me, oh, he'd get so angry because there was only so far he could put his penis inside me. And his hand would cup my penis, try to get it hard, but it was so small, and never erect because by then, I could disassociate, and it gave me the power to keep myself from responding.

He told the congregation that his chore was a burden, but it was one he was willing to bear, the only way to cleanse me. It was no more a burden to him than it was to my father. There was lust in his eyes. When I turned eleven and my breasts started to grow, he was like a starving wolf. No matter where I was, he'd find me in my hiding places, down through the woods past my house, up in trees. Everywhere I ran, he found me, then he'd sodomize me and he'd make me do the same to him. He couldn't stop. Then he got angry because what I had was too big to be a clitoris but too small to be a real penis. He wanted something big. He wanted something that could penetrate him, but my penis had stopped growing by then. In another year I'd menstruate, but it wouldn't last long, only five years or so. In between that time I grew facial hair, I grew taller, and my shoulders widened, but all that stopped too. My underarm hair grew, my leg hair, pubic hair, it was all there, fine, not coarse, all in its proper place but not completely developed. Like the rest of me it failed to form.

My questions did not have simple answers. The first wasn't the most obvious. Not, Who am I, but What am I? Is there a right way to be male or female? A masculine pronoun was

selected for me, but is my gender already chosen as well? Are
there gender roles I'm supposed to follow? What are they, how
am I supposed to act, who's going to teach me?

By the time I was twelve I had tried to kill myself twice.
Once by strychnine. Once by overdose. I wasn't found and
then saved, I was alone and then woke up. At thirteen, I left
after many more attempts. I left because I was on the verge
of killing not just myself, but someone else. I left because I
wasn't sure where I belonged. What I looked like didn't match
how I felt. I didn't know how to experience myself as totally
male or totally female. I felt like a fraud. What we look like
on the outside affects how we feel on the inside. It happens
to everyone. But the difference is, the outside and the inside
usually match. Mine didn't. I had a little of everything. One
testis, one ovary. Breasts, facial hair. Vaginal opening, penis. I
had a little of everything and that made me a nothing. I didn't
just quietly cross the boundaries, I crashed through them in the
most violent way a person can go. There was no one there to
help me back over, they were trying to crucify me for a sin that
wasn't my own. There was no comfort in my body. The outside
attacked the inside, reshaping it, and I had no choice but to
make myself invisible.

Sometimes when people refer to me as a he, I have to remind myself that it's me they're talking to or about. I don't
really know how to be a *he*, but I watch other men and I do the
best I can.

You ask who knows about my condition, about this shame
I live with. I've shared it with one person, and he has never
betrayed me. He's the only one who has ever been able to say
the word without shunning or hurting me. He's the only one I
have ever known who hasn't made me into carnival folklore.
I've tried hard not to think about us because this is one let
down I won't be able to live with, but lately I've been wondering
if you'll always be able to treat me like that too.

"Danny."

I open my eyes. The back of my head, shirt, and jeans are

soaked through. The sky has clouded over, the stars have disappeared, the past is gone.

"Darlin', you need to rest comfortably."

"I'm fine here," I say stubbornly, though everything inside me aches to be on friendly terms again.

"Come on, Danny. You're making this very difficult for me. I've never had a first fight with anyone. You know what to do better than I."

I turn to him. Not him. No, I won't use that pronoun anymore, no matter how awkward it is or sounds. I turn my head to look at Jesse.

"Our first fight," I repeat. A first dance, a first kiss, it stands to reason that a first fight is to be expected at some point.

We climb into the sleeper and I pull Jesse's face toward mine but then there's yet another surprise. Jesse pushes me on the bed and falls on top of me. The roundness and flatness of this body is so goddamned contradictory that I could come with the pleasure of just knowing it's on me. We kiss for less than ten seconds yet it feels like weeks, months, years.

"If only I could lasso time, go back and make everything right for you. I wish I could heal all your wounds."

"In a small way you have."

"Are there others like you out there?" The question tumbles out before I can stop myself.

"'Others like me'?" Jesse parrots, which proves I'm still viewed as one of them, and rightly so after that comment.

But now it's too late. I can't pretend I didn't ask it.

"Other hermaphrodites?" I whisper.

Jesse sits up, then doubles over, as if I've stabbed through the skin and into the soul with that word. I caress Jesse's shoulders, down the spine, looking for the injury.

"In medical texts with our legs pried apart, our eyes blackened out, with fingers holding up our misshapen phalluses, measuring tapes held up against abnormally small penises or shockingly large clitorises," Jesse snaps.

"I mean living, breathing people, not books."

"That's how I finally found out about myself, you know. I searched medical libraries until I saw a photograph of something like me. I eventually went to a doctor and he found that I had both an ovary and a testis. A 'true' hermaphrodite, he said. A congenital eunuch. He'd never seen anything like me. He wanted to take pictures, call in others because I was a freak of nature. He said, 'You can't live with this deformity. It's not normal. You'll have to have reductive surgery. It's possible there will be nerve damage, but it's better to look normal than have feelings. Most women don't enjoy intercourse anyway, so it won't be a true loss.' I imagine there must be others out there, I can't be the only one, can I?" Jesse asks as tears drop off the edge of the eyelids.

"What happened to you after you left?" I ask, pulling Jesse down into my arms. This is the most body-on-body contact Jesse has ever allowed, so I scarcely breathe for fear of making Jesse aware we're completely against each other.

"No more, not tonight," Jesse says.

"You're right. No more tonight. Sleep, Jesse. You're safe here with me. I promise I won't let anything happen to you. Never again."

Always knock on wood.

"Punch Bug," I say, giving Jesse's arm a powerful smack.

Jesse rubs the muscle and says, "What'd you hit me for?"

"There's a Punch Bug," I declare, and point to the Beetle ahead of us. "Didn't you play that game as a kid?"

Even as I ask, I know the answer. Our hands come together and we both squeeze. We've done that a lot lately.

About twenty minutes later Jesse hauls off, punches my bicep. "There's a HOG!" Jesse calls excitedly.

"Beetles only, you brute," I say, rubbing my arm.

"Well, hell. It's a nice-looking bike, anyway."

"What's that, an '87?"

"That, my friend, is a 1990 Custom Softail. She's a beauty, isn't she?"

"I think it's an '87."

"Don't challenge me, Danny. I know my Harley's."

I smile like a proud parent. "How'd you ever come to afford those bikes. And the bar for that matter?"

Jesse sighs and stares out the window. I only make it worse by asking, I know, but I need to—want to know.

"Do you know what it's like to starve?" Jesse asks. "I don't mean going a day with just one meal but days without so much as a lick of something salty, or sugary, or chocolatey?"

I shake my head. I've never suffered the way Jesse has.

"I left Alabama at thirteen for a world I knew I was going to starve in, yet I still chose it, because nothing could be as bad as where I was. I slept in unlocked cars and dug through dumpsters for food. Hell, I fought mangy dogs for something as small as an apple core because I was starving, and it was still better than where I came from. Eventually I made my way to North Carolina, and you know transients—that's what I'd become—transients all go to the same places, the rundown sections of cities, which is where I went. There were people on the lookout for homeless kids like me. You want to make a buck for a cigarette or a candy bar, come in here, take your clothes off for some businessman, let him look at you, masturbate, and be on his way.

"There must've been ten of us sitting in this alley searching for scraps or pennies. Sure enough this fella came 'round, said he was looking for some fresh meat. This strip joint didn't usually get busted because it was where the rich businessmen came to. It was very hush-hush, so what did we have to lose? They wanted us to wear masks, because our faces weren't important, and they didn't want us reminding them of their teenage kids at home. They just wanted to see our bodies. Six others went. One boy persuaded me to go because, when you're desperate, you'll do anything for food, or a place to sleep, or for the truly hopeless, a drink, and a cigarette.

"We were each given a cubicle, partitioned off with a particle board, so we could hear what was going on around us.

We put our masks on and a man would come into the cubicle, take his pants down and do his thing. Sometimes they'd ask for oral pleasure, and they'd toss another ten bucks at us, but what they didn't know was that the owner came in and took nearly everything we made. I wouldn't touch any of them. I'd stand there for them, and I'm sure this won't come as a surprise, but that was more than enough. To get a good look at my grotesque body. What a fantasy: all in one. Sometimes the men would stay long enough for two rounds. Word got around that a carnival freak was on display, so I got rather popular.

"After several weeks, I began to notice the same guy comin' round. First once a week, then a couple times, then every night. One night, I left at about two-thirty, and went searching for a place to sleep. We had to change our alley every few days or we'd get mugged. Imagine that, one poor man robbing another. I noticed a limo following me, and was scared, so I just kept my hands in my pockets and kept my head down. It finally pulled up and stopped. The window rolled down and there he was. He said, 'It's you, isn't it,' because he'd never seen my face. He said, 'You come with me and you won't have to do this anymore. I'll get you some clean clothes, and good food, and all the cigarettes you want. You deserve better, don't you?'

"You know why I went? Not because I was cold and hungry, or because I hadn't slept in a real bed in almost a year. I went because he spoke kindly to me. I got in the limo and I sealed my own fate. We struck up a bargain. There was a small cottage, an old servant's house just on the edge of his property. I was to live there, never show my face because he had a nice pretty wife, a handful of children. I said fine, as long as I was out of the rain and the cold, as long as I had food and water and cigarettes. But we had to seal the deal, so I bent over his lap in the limo and did what he wanted.

"I spent months there, locked in, doing nothing but reading, ten, twelve hours a day. The only time I could go outside was at night when he came 'round to see me. It was usually every night, unless he was out of town. He was a very wealthy man, an attorney from what I gathered. When I'd hear the lock click and he'd come in, I'd strip, and he'd do his thing. There was never any touching, other than the first night in the car."

"Why?" I ask.

"Well, he was a smart man. He knew politics was in his future. Why get caught? If there was no physical contact, technically he'd done nothin' wrong. All I had to do was lie on a bed, or sit in a chair, or stand next to him, and he'd talk and masturbate and that was it. What a way to fulfill your fantasy.

"Then one night I told him I wanted to go, that I was ready to move on. I'd been there about ten months or so. He said I was an ungrateful freak of nature, that he was going to call the authorities, tell them I'd been squatting, have me thrown in jail. Told me I was better off where I was because people weren't ready to live side-by-side with a monster. He said he was going away for a few days, taking his family, and I was to sit and think about all he'd given me. Go hungry, so I'd remember what living on the streets was like.

"It wasn't that difficult breaking out. The windows were barred, but I managed to break out a window on the back door, climb out that way. I was leaving with what I came with, nothing, 'cause he'd taken all my money. It wasn't much to be sure, but it was something. Before leaving I broke into his nice three-story mansion and stole only what was his, jewelry, money, change, gold cufflinks, anything I could carry in a duffle bag. He had wads of cash hidden in his desk drawers and in coffee cans, I swear, Danny, in places that didn't seem possible.

"Once I hocked everything, I had near ten thousand in cash. I was just about sixteen. I got myself a job in a tobacco field, slept in the field and saved. By the time I was eighteen and had left for South Carolina, I had enough to buy the bar. It was empty and in shambles. I lived there and fixed it up, while working at a gas station pumping gas. By the time I turned twenty-one it was ready to open. Gary was a teenager, he was living just down the road a piece, and he'd come in and help me out, make a few bucks here and there. He was the first friend

I ever had. Smart as a whip. The only person who knows the business better than him is me. Of course, I taught him everything I know." Jesse smiles. "One day I'm going to get him his own fast-food place or gas station so he can start a life of his own. I think he feels obligated to me. After all he's done for me, he deserves something he can call his own."

We both smoke and wait for the air to clear. Then Jesse says, "I did what I had to survive, and that's all, Danny."

"You don't need to tell me that, Jesse. What happened to the man?"

Jesse smiles again, this time with a hint of disapproval. "I see him now and again on the television. I'm sure he's doin' a fine job in the Capitol building in Washington, DC. Everyone has secrets, huh, Danny?"

Over the course of eight weeks, we go back to South Carolina three times, only staying overnight so we can get longer, hotter, cleaner showers, and a softer bed. Every time we go back, Jesse barges through the doors of the Yellow Submarine as if we've been gone for years. Gary rushes at Jesse like a worried parent, and fusses.

It's good to be back, we both agree. For a couple days, Jesse sort of flits around the bar, straightening already straight chairs, picking up unnoticeable stray trash. Jesse's mind is still in the rig, on the road, and it's made for a very happy-go-lucky person. I've finally given something to someone without getting anything in return. It feels rewarding. The word makes me laugh.

We're alone so I come up from behind and put my hands around Jesse's stomach. Jesse turns and kisses me, right there, not caring that anyone could walk in. I can't stop smiling or blushing.

"How're you feeling, darlin'?" Jesse asks, and nibbles lightly at my neck.

"I feel as fine as frog hair," I say, giving my best southern accent.

Jesse laughs and hugs me tighter.

"I haven't thanked you, yet."

"For what?" I ask.

"The trip, for putting up with me, for, I don't know, Danny, for showing me how to live a little. I wanted to get you something to show you how much I appreciate your attention. The first thing I thought of was jewelry, but you don't wear any other than this," Jesse says, touching Bobby's cross. We move to the dance floor, and dance to "The Long and Winding Road." Jesse is more sentimental than I'd have ever guessed. "Then I thought maybe some flowers or a big stuffed teddy bear," Jesse teases and I laugh.

"Or a Harley," I tease back.

"I'll get you anything your heart desires."

"Just you, Jesse."

We walk together to Jesse's apartment and sit on the couch. It's dark, though there are candles burning everywhere. My knees go weak; it doesn't even need to be sex, as long as we're close and kissing. Jesse's arms open for me. I sit with my legs across Jesse's lap, hoping to feel an erection, but there's nothing big enough to feel under the jeans. Jesse turns my face and we kiss. Fingers fumble with the button of my jeans, so I stand up and shed them. A hand inches up my thigh, and I spread my legs. You've never done this before, I think, and feel proud that I'll be the first. Jesse is still so uncertain. I take a finger and move it into me, then another. Jesse's thumb butts up against me and we both move into and out of it for so long, and I try to move so Jesse can feel everything beneath those heavy jeans.

I want to rip Jesse's clothes off. I grip the shirt collar and wrap it around my head so my face is buried in Jesse's neck. After a while Jesse squirms and tries to pull away, but I won't let go. I'm stronger than I look. I'm leaving my mark so people know this body is off limits to everyone but me. Jesse's hand is still between my legs, fingers still inside me. Let's just stay like this forever, I want to say.

Jesse's lips are puffed, bitten. Did I do that? Jesse's collar is torn. And that? The neck is bruised. I've left a circle of saliva.

I take Jesse's wet hand and draw a circle around my nipple. The two middle fingers go into Jesse's mouth, and then I pull them out and suck on them myself, then we put our tongues out and twirl them together. Then, I fall asleep. I feel myself floating, and when I open my eyes, we're in Jesse's bed. I fall asleep for the first time in my life with someone's arms around me.

eros

the combined physical and emotional expression of sex

Jesse asked me to wait, and I have. One full day. Whereas two months ago I would have paced the room with apprehension and expectation, this is different. I've waited with ease, with comfort, and with controlled excitement. I've used the time as a twenty-four-hour meditation, a twenty-four-hour mental foreplay.

Now, with my eyes closed, Jesse leads me across the hall, and I hear the door to the room open. I know its sound. But tonight, it sounds new, and its newness is inviting. When my eyelids flutter to peek, Jesse whispers, "Not yet," and squeezes my hands. Jesse closes the door, and then asks me what I see.

Again, I start to open my eyes but Jesse says, "Let your soul see for you."

After a moment of letting my ears listen and my face feel, I say, "There're candles burning."

"How do you know?" Jesse asks, pleased with my answer.

"Because I can feel their heat."

"Their wicks are too small," Jesse teases.

"Then it must be your heat," I say.

Jesse is taken off-guard, and begins to embrace me, but the shame of what Jesse thinks I'll think is stronger. If not space, then words between us. Always something. I know Jesse that well.

"What else?" Jesse says.

My hands roam Jesse's face. The pads of my fingers are keenly aware of each curve, of each crevice. Because there are so few, I know where each whisker presses through the skin. I know the breeze of the eyelashes blinking, the crook of the earlobe, and the number of wispy, nearly invisible blond hairs that encircle it. I am familiar with the curvature of these lips, the oblong roundness of the nostrils; every inch of Jesse is sacred.

No matter how hard Jesse tries to fight it, after thirty-three years Jesse wants to be discovered and adored. And Jesse wants to desire; no, desire isn't strong enough: Jesse wants to crave another body.

I imagine Jesse must be watching, but when my fingers wander to the eyes, the lids are down. Jesse is in a vulnerable state, wide open, and I waste no time coming in for the kill. My lips are like fangs against the cheek. Jesse flinches and tries to pull away, but like a snake I've wrapped myself around my prey and have to keep from squeezing it to death.

"Please, Jesse," I plead.

"It's not that I don't want to," Jesse whispers, nearly defeated by my persistence and the body's own needs. We're both aware that the argument is weakening. "You really can't imagine what's beneath all this."

Wonder, beauty, I'm sure of it, but saying it won't make Jesse believe I mean it, and it certainly won't make Jesse think differently. So, because my mouth doesn't possess the skills to soothe or heal, I let my fingers speak.

Through Jesse's hair, over every bone and muscle in the face, down the flannel of the shirt, they assure Jesse that I am not like the others who violated, who made Jesse ashamed, who made Jesse feel like a monster. I can't deny that what I want is physical and selfish. I want to be the first to give pleasure. I want to be the first to be pleasured by Jesse. But it's more than that. I want to be the one to save Jesse.

Jesse's head shakes as if hearing my thoughts.

"I can't imagine not worshipping what's beneath all this," I say, and carefully unbutton and remove the flannel shirt. "But it isn't about making love with just this," I insist, touching my own body, and Jesse's. "It's about making love with this and this." I point to our hearts and our heads. "It's not about the sex, it's about everything that surrounds it."

"You deserve a physical relationship with someone who's whole. You won't be able to overlook what's there."

"I don't want to overlook what's there; I want to rejoice in it."

"It won't be the same as men you've been with."

"We'll change the meaning of making love, then."

It's easier to buckle under my persistence than to live with my harassment, so Jesse falls into me.

I back us slowly to the bed, so slowly it doesn't feel like we're moving. Jesse's gone slack in my arms, groaning into my neck as if to say, I'm ready. I've found a way to strip Jesse's feelings of inadequacy and revulsion by lightly kissing and adoring.

"It's okay," I whisper, when Jesse fumbles with my shirt. I kiss each fingertip and say, "It's just us now. Just me and I'll never hurt you."

Little by little, Jesse removes my clothes. I'm naked for a long time, while Jesse kisses and explores, before my hands slip underneath the white T-shirt. I don't know what reaction to expect, but Jesse has become an ally, and aids me in removing the armor. I lean above Jesse's body and look down at two small breasts. They are a tiny bit flatter than mine. I cup them against my palms and let my forehead drop to the breastbone so that I can worship them. They feel as though they were molded for my hands, and my hands alone.

"Slopes," I say into skin.

Go slow, they remind me.

Move over me gently, they whisper.

And that's exactly what I intend to do.

Jesse's eyes open but can't stand the sight of my admiration.

"It's a beauty I've never known," I say.

Jesse's head turns to the side and stares at the burning wick. Is this the look of disassociation? I wonder. I look back down at the breasts below me and let my mouth be drawn to them. I lick around and into the nipples until they are hard in my mouth. I press the rest of my body down, hoping beyond hope to feel hardness through the boxers and against my pelvic bone, and I do, but it's a small hardness. One thing at a time, I tell myself. I work back into the nipples and Jesse's body convulses in shame and arousal; it's become an all-out war.

"You're perfect," I say and inch downward, outlining the tattoo with my tongue, past the rib cage, past the stomach, but Jesse's hands are there pulling me up. I'll occupy whatever land I'm given, follow whatever lead I'm offered. I fall to my back and Jesse hesitates.

"I don't want to squash you." It hasn't occurred to me that lying on top of someone is new too.

"You won't."

I push the boxers off Jesse's hips and legs. I catch only a glimpse of the lower half of the body, before Jesse's face disappears into the pillow next to my head, before muttering, "No touching."

Impossible, I think. But I know that even in the shower Jesse's hands don't make direct contact with what's there. A washcloth alone has that privilege.

I bring Jesse's face to mine and kiss the lips, using my tongue to lure them farther into me. I spread my legs. I put my heels into the backside and force Jesse down and in. I want to feel penetration with one push, I want to feel Jesse sliding in and out of me, but I don't say that because I'm not sure it's possible. I let Jesse determine what is.

There is a flutter inside me. I raise my hips to take more, but there is no more to take, and that's what Jesse was afraid of, and pulls away. But I take Jesse back again, pressing as far into me as possible. Slight movements make Jesse shudder. You're finally feeling this, I think, so I rock my hips a little more.

My hands inch down. Hard abs, soft stomach. My hands inch down. Tight thighs, soft pubic hair. Small swollen pockets where testicles should be. I want to stroke the part that keeps Jesse from being able to relate to another body. I begin to stroke Jesse, but my wrists are grasped and pushed against the mattress, next to my shoulders, so neither of us has use of our hands. Jesse rubs against me, and it's a pleasure that lifts my shoulders off the bed. It doesn't need a name. It's about the accuracy and splendor of friction. I have never been touched in this way. It's almost too good to be real.

Jesse makes love to me like this, against me, nipples grazing mine, stomach expanding against mine as we breathe. We are palm against palm. Our fingers are clutched so solidly and so firmly against the mattress that we use them as anchors. We are forehead to forehead, nose to nose. Jesse's eyes are closed so tightly that what we're doing appears too painful to complete. But it's not long before Jesse comes.

I'm too happy to notice that Jesse has fallen off me, that the blanket is wrapped so tightly it's become a second skin. I'm too lost in what's just happened to realize that Jesse is shivering so uncontrollably that the bed rattles against the wall, that Jesse is staring, unblinking, the same way Jesse must have on the table all those years ago.

"Jesse," I say and curl myself around this new skin. "That was amazing."

But Jesse just lays there, shivering.

"Jesse, you're perfect, it was perfect. Everything about you, about us, about this."

But Jesse just lays there, staring.

From a part of me that originates deeper than my soul, I feel something new come into existence. First, it's tiny, then it becomes bigger, like a balloon outgrowing the space inside me.

"I love you," I confess with surprise. "I love you more than life. I never knew that one person could fill me as much as you do. I love you, Jesse."

The instant I say it, I feel Jesse detach, even though we're right next to each other, right against each other, my arms wrapped tightly.

"You can't." It feels as though Jesse's suddenly traveled hundreds of miles away from me. "You can't."

But I do.

absolute zero

a temperature at which all molecular motion ceases

I used to think that black was the color of death. Yet the blackness of death goes well beyond black as a color. It holds permanence; it's the black of the doorway into an ambiguous infinity. I believed in the blackness of death when Dennis was killed. Time stopped and when I looked around, I saw no color, because death immediately isolated me from color, texture, sound, scent, and taste. It's as though death breaks the laws of physics and we enter a quantum universe where we're faster than the speed of light, pausing only for sound to catch up with us. During that pause, we have a moment to examine what's happened, and what we'll do when time begins again. And that moment can make or break us.

When Jesse tried to commit suicide, I was my regular take-control self until the pause, at which point I had time to realize how dismal the truth was. My love appeared to be worse than death. Exactly one hundred and ninety-seven days after we met, fifty-eight hours after we made love, thirty-six hours after I told Jesse that I had never been in love before, but now was sure that I was, and exactly twenty-nine hours after I worked out and shared our future plans that very next morning, Jesse tried to die.

Need I go on?

I mapped out our future while Jesse slept. Jesse's birth certificate was marked Male, so we could legally get married. As far as having children, I wasn't sure, but that wasn't an immediate concern. For now, I'd sell the truck, and open a garage. We'd live at the Yellow Submarine for a while, then look into buying a house, something small and cozy. We'd plant flowers, a vegetable garden, maybe get a dog. Planning a life full of color,

I wasn't expecting the blackness that descended when time stopped.

I wasn't in the room when Jesse tried it; I was in the bar drinking a beer, smoking a cigarette, shooting pool with some trucker friends. It was late, it was smoky, it was loud. Loud, as in the music from the juke box was blaring, loud, as in the nearly one hundred people in the bar were laughing, screaming, or fighting; balls were smacking on pool tables, video games were bleeping, glasses were clanking, and people were moaning behind closed doors. Yet, I still heard the gulp of water with every pill Jesse took. I heard every one of them slide down the esophagus and splash into the stomach.

I heard it, but before I had a chance to do anything about it, I got caught in a daydream. The sounds around me made me imagine kids at a water park in ninety-degree weather, sliding down a big slide and landing with delight in an enormous pool. Then I smiled and thought about being a kid again, being taken care of by my parents; about them knowing, at the very beginning of their lives together, that they were in love. But maybe they hadn't really been in love, like Jesse and I were, maybe it had been a relationship like my previous ones, where one participant was in love and the other was not, and I wondered if that was the reason why their relationship fell apart at one point. What Jesse and I felt was much, much different, I thought, and then, well, I didn't have a chance to move on to the next train of thought because I was called to my turn at the table.

It's all clear why I didn't run to Jesse's room when I first heard the pills gliding down the throat. Sucked into a stream of consciousness that made me feel warm, happy, and normal, I gave in to it. Jesse's near death was the consequence of thinking I could lead a normal life. As though I were dreaming, a scream shattered my brain, and I dropped my stick and ran to Jesse's room.

I know I screamed when I found Jesse, whose body looked somehow longer splayed on the floor, one arm straight out, the other folded under the head, a bottle of pills spilled around the hand. I fell to the floor, lifted Jesse by the shirt collar, and screamed.

Jesse's eyes were opened, glazed, lifeless. It's too much to handle, they said. I can't love myself, let alone you. I clasped Jesse's head so hard to my chest, I left my fingerprints on the cheek. I screamed and screamed and couldn't stop. I wasn't sure I even knew how to. I screamed when Gary dragged me away from Jesse's body, screamed when the paramedics threw it, as though it were already without a soul, on a stretcher and ran off with it. I screamed as I crawled upon the floor after them, with Gary yanking me backward by the ankle. My scream gave me strength to tear away. I kept howling as two truckers held me against a wall while all the patrons watched the paramedics pound Jesse's chest to get the heart beating again. They ripped the flannel shirt off and that's when my scream gave me the strength to break free and throw myself on top of Jesse's body so no one would see what Jesse was ashamed of.

"Outside," I yelled. "Please please don't do this here."

In the ambulance they were about to attach the wires of the defibrillator but paused when they saw Jesse's breasts.

"What are you staring at? Do something," I begged angrily.

There's no such thing as dignity when the person you're in love with is dying before your eyes, especially when that person purposely tried to end it. So I screamed for my lack of control, and screamed because Jesse couldn't love me, and screamed because I'd finally found a normal life and it was taken away just like that. I screamed for the injustice of it all. They found Jesse's heartbeat about the same time I lost my voice. I was glad to give up one for the other.

Jesse was hooked up to all these wires and machines, the respirator sucking in and breathing out in a steady rhythm that in no way became a comforting sound to my ears. Everything in the room was either white or metallic, so impersonal and uncomfortable, so unlike the environment Jesse spent years building. Although we had the room to ourselves, I pulled the curtain so other visitors couldn't see in. The doctors wanted to chain those poor helpless wrists to the bed. All I had to do was scream to get them to leave.

"I won't let them do it to you, Jesse," I said, rubbing lotion over the old scars. "I won't let them trap you, I won't let them humiliate you." When no one was looking I rummaged through the bag of personal items I'd put together so I could strap the watch back over the marks. "I won't let them know your secrets. I promise," I whispered in Jesse's ear, over and over.

Gary was there, haggard but alert, mostly worried. He fussed over the already perfectly unruffled sheets. He helped me protect Jesse by talking to concerned friends in the hallway, and never letting them in. He didn't seem to mind my talking as Jesse slept. I read Jesse's book of Whitman softly, hoping Jesse was listening: "'…But each man and each woman of you I lead upon a knoll, My left hand hooking you round the waist, My right hand pointing to landscapes of continents and the public road. Not I, not anyone else can travel that road for you, You must travel it for yourself. It is not far, it is within reach…'"

I read newspaper articles aloud. There was one about literacy, that reminded me of a story I meant to tell Jesse back when we were on the road, about the time Vic asked me to help fix up his Beetle. That day he was also giving Dennis a ride home, so the three of us ended up at Vic's place. I was adjusting the fuel pump while Vic was in the house arguing with his wife, leaving me stuck with Dennis.

"Grab that shop manual and turn to the fuel system, would you."

Dennis paused before lifting the book.

"I need to know what the pushrod height should be. I think it's 0.3 inches; double check that for me."

He fanned through the book twice.

"Goddamn, Dennis," I said and plucked it out of his hands. "It's chapter six," I said and handed it to him with the pages open.

He flipped through several pages one at a time.

"Can't find it," he said.

"Look under fuel pump."

"I said I can't find it," he said and threw the book at me.

"Maybe," I now told Jesse, "that was Dennis's vulnerability. He couldn't read. That's why he didn't have a driver's license. What do you think? I didn't make a big deal about it. I didn't say anything to Vic, or anyone."

Gary said, "Jesse taught me to read."

"No kidding," I said, surprised. "Jesse taught me to love poetry."

Gary nodded. "He taught me how to run a business."

"I think you two learned that together."

Gary smirked. "Yeah, maybe. He taught me how to play the harmonica."

Jesse taught me how to love, I was about to say, but decided to let Gary have the last word.

When he slipped out for coffee I whispered, "I love you, Jesse." I only said it when Gary wasn't around. It wasn't as often as I would have liked, which was probably a good thing because those words were the hands that fed the pills into Jesse's mouth.

Like a Lamaze partner, I tried to coach Jesse back to life. Jesse was the only one who knew I'd tried the same thing for Dennis. When Jesse and I were on the road, I turned the essence of myself upside down like a garbage can, tipping it over and banging on the bottom to see what was left to flutter out. Jesse had done the same, revealing every last painful secret that had been kept hidden for all those years. I'd made a solemn promise that Jesse would never again have to shoulder the day-to-day anguish that life deals us, alone. And even as I sat on the hospital bed, I tried to think up ways to help Jesse through this pain.

But when Jesse was finally awake enough to remember the suicide attempt, I was banished from the room, from the life I'd come to look forward to. At first it was just Gary keeping me from coming into the room, then the hospital kicked me out. My last memory of Jesse is no better than that of Dennis.

Neither made eye contact, neither talked, and neither listened to a word I said.

Some nights when I'm sleeping, dreams of Jesse and Dennis get mixed up. Sometimes Dennis is the one taking the pills and Jesse is the one under the machine. No matter what the dream, I run and run, but never get any closer to either one of them. I wake up sweating, tired, crying. I wake up and hold the picture of Jesse against my heart, and I get on my knees to pray, hands clasped under my chin, that Jesse will come back to me. What do I have to lose?

take risks on your own behalf
the five freedoms

I've been on the road for two months without so much as a word from Jesse. When I'm driving, I glance at the photograph on the visor, or the one in the sleeper, when I lie down to rest; in my head, I listen to Jesse recite poetry. In fact, I've purchased Walt Whitman's *Song of Myself*, having decided to memorize parts that remind me of Jesse. I write them on Post-it notes and stick them all over Old Snort.

All I have to survive on, then, is the poem, two photographs, and memories, and that's sad. But even sadder is that the tables have turned, and I sound like my ex-lovers; even more pitiful than that, I can see that my life has become an enormous cliché. Jesse would say, of course, we all live clichéd lives, look into it, see what's on the inside, there's always something special on the inside. But I am too depressed to find the good in the bad of it.

Here's what's so difficult about the whole thing: in a year's time, Jesse and I had one intimate weekend together. Still, I go through every second of conversation, laughter, and passion we engaged in, making myself see it from every angle. I make myself feel it the same way I felt it as it was happening to me. Every second I've had with Jesse lives as present tense. We began as a word, extended into a sentence, then a poem, a book. At some point, there has to be an end, a period, to most people. Perhaps an exclamation for Jesse. For me, a question mark.

Yes, the tables have turned.

Maybe here's what's so difficult about the whole thing: it was enough to make Jesse try to commit suicide. That's not the most positive achievement to add to my résumé. So, when I'm driving, I reread what Jesse and I went through, going sentence by sentence, page by page, waiting for the indicator that the story is over—the punctuation mark that invites the reader to close the back cover and admire the author's photograph. When I close the back cover, I have Jesse's attempted suicide staring back at me.

If I were an objective person, I'd know that I'm not to blame for Jesse's action, that it isn't about me loving Jesse, it's about Jesse being able to love Jesse. It's about one's acceptance of oneself, it's about being able to celebrate one's existence. It's about championing one's self with a song, like Mr. Whitman did.

You, Jesse, I'm certain, ignored this part of Whitman's tribute to himself, and I learned it too late to say it to your face, but I will declare it for you anyway. "'Divine am I inside and out, and I make holy whatever I touch or am touch'd from...If I worship one thing more than another it shall be the spread of my own body, or any part of it...'"

In two months' time, Gary has stopped taking my calls. Jesse has asked him to, I'm sure. I'm assuming that Jesse is still alive; that's how I'd say it to Gary if given the chance, with sarcasm and bitterness. Of course, I've employed some accomplices to get me the truth. They purposely frequent the Yellow Submarine and don't leave until they either get a glimpse of or a sound from Jesse Reid. They describe Jesse as beaten, depressed. They say Jesse looks like a prematurely aged man.

Tomorrow is the first of September. I know it shouldn't matter, that I should regard it as any other day, but I can't. It's the beginning of change. The leaves will begin to turn and fall, the nights will grow colder. It's another day that I won't have seen Jesse. Last year at this time I was hypersensitive to everything around me; now, like the somberness of the month itself, I feel dead inside. My depression was at an all-time low, a couple days ago. It was so bad I made a weighty decision about my future. The decision came to me as I watched a rerun of a multi-car crash.

I was headed north and ran into a buddy on a loading dock

this one Friday in Jersey City. The problem with Jersey City is the lumpers. Lumpers are supposed to help you unload but they're always busy doing "something else." They make a point of telling you it'll take them a couple hours before they can get to you. In the everyday world, this isn't a big deal but in trucking, it's money. It means weekend layover. It means out-of-pocket spending. It means a missed load. It costs less to bribe a lumper than it does to wait until they're good and ready to help. It might be under the table, it might be illegal, but there isn't much we can do if we want to keep the freight moving.

I saw my buddy Cal at a loading dock, trying to empty his load and pick up another before it got too late. I had a feeling I'd be dead-heading, driving empty, so I called my broker, who lines up my customers, to warn him. Still, if I moved fast enough, I just might be able to grab another load, so I paid some lumpers off to help me just as soon as Cal had finished. He was hot because the lumpers had put him back by an hour or two.

Cal said, "Them fuckers." He had a cigarette bouncing from his lips, his left eye squinting to keep out the smoke.

"Don't let them get you riled. You need to go easy. Some truckers talking said there's a bear settin' under the bridge that'll shoot in the back, right?" I said, referring to a city cop with a radar detector.

"Fuckin' city kitties got too much time on their hands. I'm tired of working independent. All this lumping, switchin' brokers. I'm thinking about selling in and going with a distribution center, right?"

"Then you'll have a boss man to deal with."

Cal looked out at the yard and nodded. "Yup. But I'll have a partner, I'll have more sleep time, more time with my family. There're other things that are more important. Plus, it's easier," he said, already giving in to the idea.

Four hours later, I was heading south and I saw it. It was grisly. Two bloody, mangled bodies walked me through it step by step, so I knew. It was gruesome to watch them but comforting in its own way. I had a secret that no one else alive would ever know, except Cal.

Two fourteen-year-olds, joy riding in a stolen car, drove into the path of Cal's tractor-trailer. He was hauling 43,000 pounds of steel and hit the passenger's door. The car became airborne, landed sideways, and skidded into another car, which in turn hit another car, which in turn hit yet another car. A fourth car ran under the bed of the truck. Cal and two other people were taken by helicopter to a hospital. Cal had a broken back, the other two sustained serious injury, and the two teens were pronounced dead at the scene. Cal had to submit a blood test. It didn't matter who really started it, because truckers take the blame for everything.

I park the truck on the edge of the gravel parking lot and ask a driver to send Gary out. He's not very happy to see me. He puts his hands on his hips, he shakes his head and sighs. We each pull out cigarettes as though they're pistols.

"Jesse don't want you here."

"Do you?" I ask.

Gary shrugs. "I reckon it don't matter if I do."

"It matters to me. We were friends."

Gary nods. "You don't need me like Jesse does."

"All I've done is love Jesse."

"But he ain't ready for that."

"Jesse doesn't like pronouns."

"Well."

"Well, what?"

"It's just a small word. It makes it easier for everyone else."

But it wasn't just a little word. By using he or him, they forced something on Jesse that Jesse didn't relate to.

"You disrespect Jesse. You strip Jesse of identity."

Gary gives a small shrug.

"How's Jesse doing?" I ask.

"He's improving slowly. The depression is getting better. He misses you, if that's what you want to hear, and I think he's more depressed because you're not around, but he won't admit it."

"Then let me come in."

Gary shakes his head. "It needs to be his decision."

That's the closure I came to hear. Nothing will change until Jesse learns how to love what's on the inside as well as the outside. I pull an envelope out of my back pocket and hand it over.

"What's this?" he asks.

"It's a deed. I bought a small place on the ocean for Jesse. It's nothing spectacular. As a matter of fact, it's kind of a shack, but Jesse's good at fixing things up."

"How did you afford it?" he teases.

I jab my thumb at the truck behind me. "I sold her."

"Old Snort?"

"Not Old Snort anymore."

"She was how you made your living."

"Yeah, money'll be tougher to come by. I have to pay the company for the use of the truck. I'll have a small loan for that, but so what. There are other things that are more important," I say, stealing Cal's reasoning.

"I never thought I'd hear you say that."

"Well, I've changed. All these years I've been driving, so many people have told me I was running from something, I started to believe it. But then, after I met Jesse, I started to think maybe I was running toward something. I actually thought I'd found a place to settle down. It was never about the trucking as much as it was about doing something I loved. So, I started to dream a little. I thought, I could buy that old garage right down there, fix it up and open a shop, marry Jesse, live in one place. Ordinary stuff that happens to people not like me."

Gary nods—it's a nod that tells me there's no good answer to all this—and taps the edge of the envelope against his knuckle.

"Why'd you buy him a house? Why not another Harley?"

It just goes to show how much better I know Jesse than anyone, even Gary.

"'You sea! I resign myself to you also...I behold from the beach your crooked inviting fingers, I believe you refuse to go back without feeling of me, We must have a turn together...'"

"Hmm," Gary says. "You also decide to become a scholar in those dreams of yours?" He presses the envelope and says, "What else is in here?"

"Jesse'll know," I tell him.

It's a rock from the sea with all its appendages intact.

Gary doesn't understand any of this, but in the end, it doesn't matter if he understands as long as Jesse does.

You will understand, I think, because it's been your wish all along, to go back to the unclean waters from which you think you've come.

'but the two together make me'
Great Expectations, Charles Dickens

Agnes has died.

Harry found her sitting on the couch, her head resting back against a pillow. Horace was next to her, mewing as though his heart were broken. Harry called Buzz, weeping as though his heart were broken.

Though I didn't find out until after her funeral, I drive up anyway. When I arrive at my old apartment, Harry is sitting on the steps of the house waiting for me.

"Door's unlocked," he says, sniffling.

I go in. Everything is the same, but different. There are two photos I've never seen before. One of me standing by my rig, when it was mine, the other of me and Agnes. I have my arm around her thin shoulders. She's holding Horace, the jealous bastard. Deena had forced her to pose for the picture the day I left, a year ago. One full year. She pretended she was indignant, but when I look closely, I see she has a small smile on her face, like she'd used some reverse psychology to get me into the photo. Maybe she was as comforted by my touch as I was by her spitefulness.

"Harry," I call.

He won't come into the house, so I have to go outside. He's got his face buried in a handkerchief. I sit next to him and pat his knee.

"The doctor said she died peacefully."

I nod.

"He said she probably just fell asleep and didn't wake up."

I nod again.

"It was like she knew. She surrounded herself with things."

"How do you mean?"

"There was a crucifix on the arm of the couch."

"That's spooky."

"Yeah, but I buried her with it. I thought maybe that's what she wanted. She had one of my flannel shirts over her knees like a blanket that was keeping her warm." He starts to cry again so I pat his knee some more. I'm worthless in these situations. "That container of macadamia nuts you sent for her birthday was in her lap. Her hand was still in it."

"The salt probably shot her blood pressure up," I say, and shake my head.

"Man, she loved them things. You'da thought you sent her a box of gold."

"Doctor told her to go easy on the nuts. I knew I shouldn't have sent them, but there were so few things she really loved."

"She didn't care what you sent her, as long as she heard from you. She'd stand at the door all morning, waiting for the postman. She had all your letters on the coffee table too. You might want to take them."

We have two conversations running, neither of us listening to the other, so we shut up and watch as Horace approaches us. He meows loudly, like he's protesting, like we're blocking him from seeing Agnes.

"Will you take care of him?" I ask.

Harry puts his hand out and the tip of Horace's nose bumps against his fingertips. Once he feels safe, Horace purrs and rubs against Harry's knee, something Horace has never done to me.

"We get along good," Harry says. Horace mews in agreement.

"What'll you do now?"

Harry seems uncomfortable. He scratches his closely shaven chin and sighs. Suddenly I'm aware that his face is shaven. I'm even aware that he looks thinner. His hair is combed, his clothes clean and ironed. Agnes changed him. It was easier to buckle than it was to live with her harassment.

"There's a big envelope on the kitchen table with your name on it. Agnes left it there. It's sealed."

I go back into the house and scoop up the letters I wrote once a week, repeating the things I told her on the phone every other day, and sent her packages the days I didn't call. Harry seems to think it meant something to her; my spirits lift, knowing that. I take the envelope, which is heavy, and the letters, and tell Harry I'm heading over to the cemetery.

I stop first for flowers. Agnes loved flowers as much as she loved Horace. But the mound of dirt is already covered. Once, when one of her friends died, we stayed at the grave site after everyone left and distributed flowers to other graves. She told me her friend would have wanted her to do it; she even took one for herself. She said the woman hated to see people left out. So, I leave the flowers I've brought in the truck, and then dole out ten different planters to other people's graves. Agnes would've wanted all the flowers for herself, to show how important she was. We would've argued about it. I win this one. "See, Agnes?" I say to the sky. "You taught me some manners."

I get back in the rig to leave, but I don't know where to go. Jesse is done with me, Agnes is gone, Buzz is distant because I've been gone so long. I decide to open the envelope, see what belittling thoughts Agnes left me with. The thought of her surliness actually makes me smile. She's wrapped it in so much tape, I'm expecting top secret documents. I have to use my pocketknife to slice through it.

I dump the contents on the passenger seat. Mixed in with my letters is a big ugly crucifix. Jesus, I think, staring down at it. It's heavy, it's metal, it's, I don't know, just there. I can't even get myself to pick it up. Then I notice her rosary. This I do pick up and finger. Once white, it's now dirty from use. It was something Agnes kept with her at all times.

"Okay, Agnes. You win this one," I say hanging it from my mirror and giving it a push. It swings steadily back and forth. The crucifix is still taunting me from the seat. Clearly, I can't throw it away. Clearly, I can't keep it. I'm in a real fix here.

I sift through the envelopes and find one that has Danny written on it in her spidery hand. Here we go, I think.

Danny,

Just so you know I didn't leave you the house. Harry paid me a hundred dollars for it. The agreement was I would live in it until my death. It's called a living lease. If you're reading this then I'm dead and Harry's living in the house. Don't harass him. He's probably having a hard enough time as it is. He cries a lot. If you had stayed, I would have done the same thing for you, but you left. I know I hassled you about it, but I wanted you to have some stability. Harry's doing a lot better now. He got a steady job with the county, he pays all his bills, and he's good with his kids. He isn't a bad catch, you know.

Make sure someone good takes care of Horace. Horace doesn't like you, so it better be someone else. Plus, I don't want him driving around in a truck. He has more class than that.

Make sure you do something useful with the cross. I found it at a yard sale, and thought you might like it, ha ha.

Make sure you take care of yourself. If you insist on driving that truck, at least be safe about it. You're a good girl, Danny. I think someone very special out there has fallen in love with you. You don't have to worry so much about not having childbearing hips. Nowadays you can't even see the scar from a C-section. My friend Ella's granddaughter showed me hers.

I cherished everything you gave me, Danny. You were more of a granddaughter to me than my own. I left you a good bit of cash, but the rest goes to the church. I also left you my china for when you get married. I have a feeling you won't have a proper wedding so it's the least I could do.

One last thing. I never told you I loved you because I knew you didn't want me to. It wasn't something you wanted to hear, but you knew it deep down. Here's something you do need to hear. You need to do two things

before you die: 1) Pray. 2) Let yourself be loved.
God Bless you, Danny Fletcher.

Agnes.

P.S. If you throw away that crucifix, I'll haunt you.

"You old bat," I yell at my roof, and then laugh. When I
stop, I say quietly to the letter, "You could have told me you
loved me. I would've acted like I minded, but I wouldn't have."

I start the truck and then drive down roads I used to plow,
down roads I used to oil, down roads I had sex on. The extent
of my life in this town. Destroying, fixing, destroying.

I'm heading toward Bishop Road. No matter what turn I
make, it takes me in that direction. The closer I get the more
I sweat. The more I sweat the harder I shiver. I approach the
spot slowly, as if I'm trying to sneak up on it. I park and stare.

"Here we are," I say.

I wait for Dennis to appear, the way the rest of them have
over the course of the year. I concentrate hard, as though I can
conjure up his spirit.

"Come on," I demand. "Come on, here I am. This is what
you've wanted."

I get out, and march angrily toward where he should be.
And that's when I realize. There's nothing for him to come to,
no picture or memorial, no flowers or wooden cross. No one
thinks about him when they pass this spot, as they pass this
spot right now, as I'm standing here staring at it. If it had been
me, would it have been any different? I turn to face the road.
Cars drive by yet no one looks.

"What about Dennis!" I shout, as the next car approaches.
"Why won't you look! Why don't you mourn his death! What
did he die for?"

I run to the truck and search through my toolbox for a hammer and nail. Tossing envelops on the floor, I grab the crucifix.

"How about now?"

I hammer it to the tree, hitting my thumb twice, but the pain
doesn't stop me. When my thumbnail turns black, I'll wonder

how it happened. "Doesn't anybody remember?" I stand in the middle of the lane so a car can't pass. Moving quickly to the driver's window, I say, while wielding my hammer, "Do you remember the man who died here?"

The woman tells me I'm a lunatic, rolls her window up, and then manages to drive around me without running over my foot. I make the next car stop and ask her. "What did he die for?" They don't know and they don't care.

I throw the flowers down upon the twigs and weeds, under the crucifix, then look out at the road where people go about living their lives. How dare they!

No one stops long enough to answer. I yell into the air around me, "What did he die for?"

"You," the voices call back. They come from every direction, from every road, from every state. Thousands and thousands of dead voices, a choir of harmonious answers. "So you could live," they say.

"Well, I didn't fucking ask him to!" I yell back and fall to my knees where he died, then cry into my hands.

I stop at a pay phone and call Buzz.

"Hey," I say. My nose is so stuffy I feel as though the sound is coming out of my ears. I have to squat because my knees are banging together, because I'm no longer strong enough to even carry the weight of my own life. Good thing you got out when you did, Jesse, I think.

At first Buzz doesn't answer and I'm instantly terrified that I've really lost him too.

"I really want to see you guys before I leave," I say quickly.

"You're definitely leaving again."

"What's here for me?" I ask him.

He's silent. I've offended him.

He says, "We had a family meeting."

"And you guys decided you don't want to see me?"

"The kids thought Barley would be a good companion for you."

I'm choked up again. "I can't take him, Buzz. He's too much a part of your family."

"It's something the kids really want. So do I, so does Deena. We worry about you out there alone. You going to come by?"

"Yes," I say.

"What would you like your going away dinner to be?"

I stop and think. I think about the span of my entire life up till now. I've come to the point where the dead and living have met, a point of rebirth.

"Eggs," I tell him.

"Eggs? What kind of eggs?"

"Any. Scrambled, hard boiled, sunny side up. You decide."

Before I go to Buzz's to pick up Barley, I drive back to Agnes's. Harry isn't there. I fish the key out from under a rock and slip back in. Propped up against the table lamp is the photograph of me and Agnes. I take it, along with a photo of when she was younger, then I steal a roll of tape. In the sleeper box I start pasting. I paste up photos and notes and a Yellow Submarine matchbook. Just like the scrap books the girls in high school used to put together. There's one of Buzz and me in our plow, the flame on the front quarter-panel fiery red. The two of Agnes, photos of my parents and me, and of Bobby. It's time I begin to celebrate my life, to put together my scrap book, to open the borders rather than crash through them. My life had to die before it could come back to life again.

Okay, then, I'm back.

Once I'm satisfied with the decorations, I make room in the passenger seat for Barley. One after the other I stuff the things Agnes gave me back in the envelope. Mixed in with everything is a postcard of the ocean in Jesse's handwriting. Jesse must have sent it to Agnes's, knowing I'd be there at some point or other. It occurs to me that if she hadn't died, I wouldn't have gotten it.

She died for you, I hear in my head.

As I try to quiet the voices, the paper stings my fingers,

reminding me that Jesse has written. I'm so anxious I nearly hyperventilate, but calm myself down long enough to read it:

> You will hardly know who I am or what I mean,
> But I shall be good health to you nevertheless,
> And filter and fibre your blood.

> Failing to fetch me at first keep encouraged,
> Missing me one place search another,
> I stop somewhere waiting for you.

Mr. Whitman comes to rescue me—us. I try to pick out the one word that tells me Jesse does love me, that Jesse loves me enough not to want to die. That life, well, not just life, but life with me is worth living. But even as I pinpoint first one word and then another, I keep coming back to this one thought. I remember when Jesse showed me a painting with people standing in a park. Jesse taught me about pointillism, explaining that each dot on its own was just a dot, that if you stared at it up close the dots began to stand out on their own, but when you looked at them from a distance, no matter what color or size, the dots merged into one, that each was a very powerful part of the whole. So, I decide not to look at Jesse as already complete, but at the two of us as very important parts of the whole. I decide not to look for the one word that gives me my answer because the answer is in the message. I won't try to figure out who or what has led me to this point in my life, because everyone: me, my parents, Bobby and Dennis, people I have met and will meet, and even Jesse are all a part of the same picture. Jesse and I can be one, and still be independent. Bobby taught me that it was important to be true to the things you loved, that you had to fight for them no matter what it costs. And that's just what I'm going to do.

It's good news, for sure, and yet…and yet…

I sit and hold the postcard in my lap and wonder about all those lost souls out there who beg, unnoticed, unheard, for release. I wonder now if by unbinding Dennis from this place, from me, they, too, will feel as if they've been untethered from their final places. I wonder if they are watching me, waiting for me. I wonder which of them, if any, will try to keep me from finding Jesse, or which, if any, will point me straight to the spot where Jesse waits.

Acknowledgments

It seems near impossible to acknowledge and thank everyone who, over the past decade or so, helped bring this novel to life, but I'm going to give it my best college try. First and foremost, my parents and sister and the rest of the family. Those who mentored me over the years: Leigh Allison Wilson, this would never have happened if you hadn't told me good or bad, just do it; and Susan Richards Shreve and Richard Bausch, thank you for holding the bar so high. Jon Card for sharing his trucking stories with me, and for answering every strange question I threw at him. My Friday card group especially Julia Fuleihan, Marjorie Julian, and Pat Wilson who gave the book a careful and analytical read. Stephanie and John Vanderslice, whose critical eyes helped mold *Knit* into what it is today. And the best dynamic duo in the publishing world, Jaynie Royal and Pam Van Syk. From the bottom of my heart, thank you for believing in this.